Time Passages

A Short Story and Poetry Collective

J.A. Terry

Pandora's Boox

Some of the events described happened as related; others were expanded and changed, while others are complete works of fiction. Some of the individuals portrayed are composites of more than one person, and many names and identifying characteristics have been changed as well.

Published by
PANDORA'S BOOX
www.pandorasboox.org

ISBN: 978-0-9763122-0-8

Printed in the United States of America

TABLE OF CONTENTS

"Some of us put up walls not to keep others out; but to see who cares enough to tear them down."

-Unknown

Time Passages

GATEKEEPER

His days are grueling, exhausting – mile after mindless mile – with people he wouldn't look twice at, let alone travel with – and he wakes up hating the world. Knowing exactly what he wants, what needs to be done – to fulfill his life's calling, leave his mark on the world; attain the success foretold him, yet uncertain in the path that will open the door. And then there she was, waiting at the gate – longing to soothe his anxiety, with a gentle caress of her hand, ease his apprehension with her knowledge of the path – dispel his angst with her undying love, relieve his agony with her sex and lust.

"Walk this way," she whispered softly - "toward the land of the morning sun – but put on your shades, before taking my hand – lest your eyes get burned while we romp in the sand…"

Autumn Griffin

The seasons of our lives are well defined – born into winter we grow into spring – flourish in summer – mature in autumn – only to return full circle to winter – where we wind down and vanish.

I am autumn's child
I do not like it
Much
Leveling off
Maturing
Feeling like summer
Longing for
Spring

Surrounded by people
All telling me
Different things
Taking everything
They can from
Me

Places to go
Things to see
Opportunities knocking
Too many
Missed
Felling suffocated
Never so
Alone

Like the raindrop
On my
Windshield
Unmoving – unyielding
No matter
How fast I
Travel

Why does it only
Stay in one
Place
To be dried
Up
Burned alive
By the
Suns striking
Rays

I hear the
Griffin calling
From which way
I do not
Know
I no longer feel
Frightened
Perhaps at this
Moment
I'm ready to
Go –

JUNTO DE NUEVO

Quad shot latte – table for two – southern breeze softly caressing – the only ingredient missing of perfection…you. Eight years, way too long – but merely a drop in the endless bucket of life – a single grain in the sands of time – of what brought us to this moment – where misplaced hearts again unite – take flight and soar into eternity; refusing to let go – stand still or be broken.

TO THE ONE WHO KNOWS

A wanderer she has always been – sometimes lost, sometimes not –
but searching nonetheless – for the missing portion that would
connect the other half of the whole – bringing sanctity, completing
her.

This void she has always been aware – an emptiness which lingered in
the depths of her soul, leaving her longing for fulfillment she always
believed possible, but still had never known. Reaching the point in
wondering if the search were all for naught – until he crossed the
bounds of time, making his presence known.

Who was this handsome stranger come knocking at her door –
another lonely drifter seeking comfort in her words? A vagabond, a
guru, a gypsy, a tramp – she tried to push him from her mind, but her
spirit cried, alas!

Something so familiar in his essence did linger – she took a stroll
inside his mind, in an instant knowing they were two-of-a-kind – and
still her mind would not let her believe. For too many had attempted
to travel that path, claiming their connection in a fictional past.

Three simple words, "Who are you" – and suddenly visions came
rushing back. Knowing with clear certainty he cannot be an illusion –
for life surely could not deal so cruel a trick – not to have been carried
this far, for so very long, within the depths of her heart.

Onto this path she willingly stumbles, grasping for whatever shred he will give – vowing to hold strong and not lose him again. For her heart could not withstand the loss of him twice – not in this lifetime – this world, or the next...

SOAR

In this, the great symphony of life, he suddenly appears, as if from a dream – with masterful skill, leading my artistry to the fulfillment of orchestra; a perfect accompaniment to my lone harmony – his unique energy a gift – that somehow completes and brings the piece to one beautiful and perfect whole; setting my spirit free – to soar and explore the endless heights of infinity – with clear certainty never before known.

TRUTH DEFINED

I know now
Who'll be waiting
When I cross
The other side

I often thought
It him
Who had died

My spirit
Tells me
It was you
All along

Waiting patiently
To guide me
Home -

TELEPHONE

Spa day – honeydew facial – new negligee – shook her hair loose then checked herself twice in the mirror, making sure she looked just right. Then she went to him – on his turf, to make her intentions known. Something her therapist advised her to do, in order to get their relationship back in the groove.

Feeling confident and sure, she approached beguilingly – asked what he was doing, batted her eyelashes and smiled. He turned his attention her way, raised his eyebrows and smiled – reached for another boiled peanut, eyes drifting back to the race. Crushed, but refusing to let her feelings be known, she turned and walked to the bar – poured herself a Coke, then retreated to her own domain, grabbing her robe along the way.

She closed the door and dialed the number, feeling nervous as she listened to the ring. His tone was one of happiness when he recognized her voice. So glad to hear from her, having missed her – assuring her that no matter what the trouble, he was there to make everything right.

"Shall I place the charge on the credit card we have on file," he asked – as she reached over and turned off the light – always hating this part before the illusion began.

- 11 -

ENRAPTURE

She walks the extra mile to merely glimpse in his eyes – intense, unrevealing, sometimes smiling, always unnerving she tries hard to read – leaving frustrated, refusing to give up. Aggravating passivity moving too slowly – while admiring externally, she longs to make him move. In the same direction, on the same page, effortless chemistry, confounding logistics – languishing in lust, his and her own. Wanton desire, fantasies erotic, bring her to her knees – transform on a whim, darkened room, cumulative heat where shadows loom.

AGE OF AQUARIUS

She desperately needed to know the
why of it all – contemplated for
days and nights on end – reaching
inside, re-examining everything she
knew of her true self, the life she'd
lived to this point, and what little
she knew of him. The process
exhausting, as she traveled the outer
limits, pushing herself farther than
she'd ever gone – searching for
reason, but finding only one truth; a
truth whose acceptance could quite
possibly lead to insurmountable
consequences; a truth she could no
more deny than the stars in the
southern sky; a truth she'd been
seeking the whole of her life; a truth

that renewed her faith in God; a truth that made every moment of
suffering worthwhile; a truth so enigmatic that a lifetime of anguish
and shattered dreams suddenly made absolute and perfect sense – as
the road leading to such ethereal bliss, could be lined with nothing
less.

KILLING ME SOFTLY

She woke up one morning with an urgency to become more involved in her daughter's lives. I call it women's intuition – she doesn't question it or call it anything at all. That very day she signed on for Girl Scout and PTO duty, in addition to the Sunday school class she taught two days a week, and has been stretching herself thin ever since. The feeling of urgency replaced with overwhelming exhaustion – and still she's no closer to her girl's than she was before, but at least she can say she's involved.

People at work noticed a change within a few weeks, as she was sickly pale, had no energy and suffered extreme mood swings, which was not at all like her. After a few months of this routine, she started becoming sick with what she believed to be allergies, but still refused to take time off work to see a doctor – until the day she woke with sores on the back of her throat and her lips swollen with what she believed were cold sores. The doctor gave her a z-pack of antibiotic and sent her on her way – she returned to work the next day, to the horror of her co-workers, who begged her to take some time off to heal herself – but she was having none of it.

Feeling physically spent as time wore on, she somehow adjusted to her ailments and forged ahead, refusing to let anything stop her or slow her down. A few more months and it would be summer, school would be out and then she'd take a break, she kept telling herself. But something else was bothering her that wasn't so easy to shake – something unidentifiable and somewhat familiar constantly gnawing at the back of her mind – driving her on when she hadn't the energy to drive herself, not knowing what or why.

If she opened herself, looked deep inside, she would recognize that gnawing from her own childhood, brought on by a repressed memory of her father and his late night visits to her and her sister's room – the look in the eyes of her own daughters, mirroring that of hers, if she'd only find the strength to see.

And while clarity loomed on the horizon, her husband feared what was happening and knew if it came down to a choice, that it would be her that had to go, so that he could continue the life he'd built in secret with his girls.

"Honey, you look exhausted," he said as he stood in the doorway and watched her fumble with the coffee filter. He walked across the room and took it from her. "Here, let me do that, you go on and take a shower." She looked up at him and forced a smile, not having the courage or strength to tell him she hated his bitter coffee, but thankful that he'd offered to take over this simple task, which meant she had a few extra minutes to stand in the hot shower and try to wake up.

He watched as she shuffled her feet across the floor and disappeared down the hall, and then he reached into the pocket of his jeans and withdrew the vial, added a few drops in the bottom of the pot and flipped on the switch to brew.

DARK WATERS

I was shocked, but not surprised, when I read the headline and saw the clip of the familiar faces, stricken with unidentifiable emotion for the camera, as the story heading scrolled across the bottom of the screen; 4-YEAR-OLD BOY MAULED TO DEATH BY FAMILY PIT BULLS. What did surprise me was the fact that the dogs were what got him and not one of the fucked up adults he was born into the care of.

I'd witnessed their dysfunction, blatant abuse and disregard for several hours – as for one beautiful afternoon, we shared the same beach.

It started with the twin Pit predators – whenever someone walked too close to the truck they were chained to. They waited quietly as the unsuspecting victims approached and once they crossed the barrier, visible only to the dogs, they lunged – the chains rattling as they unfurled along the sand then clanging loudly once they were pulled taught and the hundred-plus-pound pits reared on their hind legs – balancing against the chains that were fastened to their spiked collars. Their incessant barks and snarls, glistening canines, eyes black with rage, and the owners laughing their asses off as the people screamed and took off running for their lives – it was positively sickening.

Then there was the child – his piercing screams causing the gulls to flee the scene and everyone within earshot to stop whatever they were doing and turn to search out the child in peril – only to find his greasy, fat father dragging him up the beach and stopping several times to beat his ass – declaring for the world to hear that he'd just done with the little fucker!

He was tossed on the sand like a wet beach towel where he continued to kick and scream. The mother finally rolled to one side and hoisted herself to her knees and struggled to stand. She took several agonizing steps toward the child – pale dimpled, rippling flab wiggling as she went, until she reached him, bent down, grabbed him by one arm and jerked him off the ground then dragged him toward the truck, his little toes skimming the sand, leaving a trail – the pits yapping and lunging as if he was a tasty morsel they were being tempted with.

I thought about getting their license number and making the call, but I didn't, because quite frankly the child protective services in Florida is riddled with abusive predators just waiting to get their hands on some poor mistreated, messed-up child – so it's hard to tell which fate was worse. So, I tried to push it from my mind, as I turned on my ipod, put on some soothing music, rolled over and basked in the warmth of the sun.

I didn't stay tuned to listen to the details of the case, but chances are the child was dead long before the mauling began – as most times the dogs strike at the throat, killing their victims fairly quickly, sometimes instantaneously. One can only hope.

KEROUAC

She stood among
The classics
Looking
But not seeing

Although Dracula
Caught her eye
Recognition was
Fleeting

She touched the
Spines
Of various sizes
Scent of mocha
Latte
Assaulting her
Senses

Suddenly he was there…

Asking what she
Wouldn't
Let her self
Wonder
But the flip side
Of the silver
Coin

From her perspective
Holding this
Connection
Having absolutely
Nothing
To do with
Books

Then again he
Asked softly
Snatching this one
From within

Have you ever
Fallen
Helplessly in
Love
With someone
That you
Have never before
Met –

QUITTING

Sunshine day
Starbucks waiting
Write alone all day

Didn't ask
If I had plans
Took off on your own

I fucking quit you

SHADOWS IN SILENCE

She wanted so much to believe; every painful step taken, leading to this moment. But in truth she knew nothing, only what she was told, uncertain of her own feelings; listening for whispered undertones; an explanation of the role she was playing, and why. The cynic inside refusing to allow total acceptance, lest she find herself once more alone; wounded on the path, mortally bleeding. For this time she was certain, there would be no return; her heart and mind so weary, from walking on the ledge. No more bittersweet memories or lies to cloud her head. It was truth she sought. What she had come to expect. What she deserved.

COME SAIL AWAY

It was a long, hot summer – each day that passed bringing her one step closer to autumn – knowing he soon would be there – brining with him, cool relief from the relentless, sweltering heat that only grew in intensity; and then there were days, like this, when she simply couldn't go a moment more without release. And so she reached for him, the only way she knew how – the one she'd come to count on – knowing exactly what she needed – always offering willingly.

She leaned back and tried to relax – her body tense in anticipation – eyes closed, wrapping herself in the sound of his voice, lost in the truth of his words – as she imagined him touching her, taking pleasure in her need and her want. She took her time, savoring each touch, each erotic caress, as she imagined he would…if he were the one doing the touching.

Her mind drifting – floating – water lapping gently – to a place she'd never been, with a man she'd never met – where together, in her thoughts, they played soft and teasingly slow, the tightening deep inside growing beyond all reason – her hips moving forward, as she

imagined him tasting her – hands in his hair, pulling him to her –
crushing her mouth to his, tasting herself greedily –
aahhh…aahhh…aahhh – he pushes away – rising above – eyes glazed
with passion – blue piercing green – he enters her hard and fast – god,
this must be heaven – she grabs his hips to pull him deeper still – her
fingers working in his place – until she can't hold it any longer and lets
herself go – calling out to him; knowing that not only can he hear
her…but he can feel her as well.

CURVES

Many things come to mind when I think of the word curves…

Long, winding back roads with their curves that took me up, over and around the countryside – music blaring, wind blowing, smoking one designer cigarette after another – mile after endless mile – searching for something – anything – all roads leading me nowhere; just one shitty town after another; each one the same once you turned off the façade of Main Street; with their taverns and whores – backwoods boys looking to score – with names like Bubba, Luke and Tex. Oh, and lets not forget Big Red…

The first time he went away and wrote for me – calling me from the mountains and waking me, to see if I'd read the email yet – so excited to be expressing himself with words – me the tutor, he the eager student. "Your green eyes sparkle like gems and your smile stands bright against your tan skin and long brown curls. Your soft touch and gentle caress excite me and bring me emotional comfort and physical pleasure. You're an old soul, with womanly curves, and a hippie style that quite frankly drives me wild."

Old soul, womanly curves, hippie style – yep, that's me. I took those words to heart, carried them with me for months, even after he left – reading them over and over until the paper began to wither and shred. In the end they were only words – and quite frankly didn't mean shit!

And then there was the curve that took the life of the one I loved first – on that dark, rainy night when all hope was lost and there was nothing left to live for. Instead of slowing he accelerated – taking his anger at me out on the road. Until the road reached up and snatched him from his misery – leaving me alone to drown in mine. Every day for years after, I had to drive that curve, no matter where it was I wanted to go. How many times I saw the scene in my mind, just as it was that night – each time my body rocked with wave after wave of shivering grief, as I rode the curve that led to my own personal hell.

CURVES…what can I say but it's a wicked fucking word.

AFTERSHOCK

They had the afterglow of morning sex written all over them – reflected on their faces and in the way he touched the small of her back as he held the door and led her through. What better way to luxuriate than throwing on some clothes and heading to Starbucks for an espresso fix – enjoying the beginning of what promised to be a beautiful day. They'd come so far in the past two years – putting an end to each others fears – bonding, reconnecting, stabilizing the foundation on which their marriage was built. He stood faithfully by her side – venti bold in hand, with extra room for ice – waiting patiently for her order to be up – then SHE walked in the door – and the mere sight of her brought it all flooding back.

He quickly took her in – all five feet seven inches – face framed with a wild mane of untamed curls that he'd buried his face and hands in on countless occasions – as she held him between her thighs and begged him for more. He could tell by looking she was straight from her bed – could feel her warmth – smell her scent – if he closed his eyes and allowed himself – the oversized peasant shirt and bellbottom jeans giving nothing away – but he knew – knew all too well what hidden treasure lie beneath.

She kept her sunglasses on, but looked him square in the eye – phone in hand – deep in conversation with her man – a million miles away, but right by her side. For the first time since he left, the sight of him didn't cause her heart to leap from her chest – she felt nothing for him – all that remained was a tinge of regret.

He turned and walked out the door – she couldn't help but smile – remembering what being in her presence did to him once upon a time – wondering if perhaps she still had that affect. Probably not, but it makes no difference these days – in fact, it never really did.

PERPETUAL WETNESS

It hangs thick in the languid air, clinging to sun-kissed flesh; sea fog roils, as they search for fulfillment, the other half would make them whole. A mystical breeze stirs, whispering promises from the sea; she stood in wait, along the shore, accepting this, its final offering. Oceans of time they traveled, wandering, always separately; rocky shores and white hot sands, leading them to now. When the rains came in torrents, washing away each painful past; blissful release it promised to bring, total completeness is what they found. As their souls met; finally merged; in a wave of passion they blend into one.

TIME PASSAGES

Time...
It passes so slowly when you're waiting; waiting for something you've searched for so long; knowing it is yours, not able to show it. Hidden behind lies, deception; reveling in truth, divine. Locked away in some secret place, no one knows but you; waiting for you to come release it – claim it for your own; if only for a moment, while promising forever. Returning to that place, where it once again waits; as time goes by, ever so slowly.

ALLURE OF SANCTUARY

She sits in a trance-like state; the sensual, ambient sound taking her deeper into melancholic sadness. The connection broken, she reached but could not find – descending from euphoric heights, and all that which is mere deception of the mind. Ethereal chants of Spanish monks deliver her into darkness – where she finds comfort in the black embrace. The truth of her soul, hers alone – not to be shared or tossed about lightly; nighttime whispers, beckons her home; the journey leaving her spent and forlorn. Nebulous void she once recoiled, as she followed the allure of sanctuary; a familiar and fearful sight. She closes her eyes, rids her mind and slips once more into eternal aloneness – that place from which she was briefly freed – she bows in silent surrender.

MY NIGHTS

Daylight fades
Sky's blue hue deepens
Sun's setting rays
Turning white clouds pink
Reflected on still waters

Alone on the dock I wait
The blanket of darkness
Falling softly around me
Moonbeams drop diamonds
Sparkling at my feet

Quiet calm settles on my world
The ugliness suddenly gone
Beauty is all I see
My soul finding peace
Always in the still of the night

DANCE OF WANDERING SOULS

She thought she was dying; the pain, *that* excruciating; the anxiety and nausea overwhelming; and the sweats; god, the sweats; unlike anything she'd ever experienced before. After twenty-four hours of suffering, she finally called her doctor and made an appointment. He examined her thoroughly, while running through the typical barrage of questions in an attempt to pinpoint a diagnosis, but kept coming to the same inconclusive end.

She asked about psychic intrusion, as there was an intense ethereal element to what was happening to her – not to mention the fact that she believed she'd recently met the mate of her soul. He looked at her like she'd lost her mind and immediately checked her chart; asking if the Zoloft was still working for her. She knew it would be futile to continue along those lines; remembering a time when she could come to him with anything; and he listened. She was suddenly saddened at the fact that he'd allowed the years and the industry to stifle his open-mindedness; and so she dropped it.

He sent her on her way with a prescription for something to ease the cramps and nausea; telling her that if the symptoms didn't go away in a few days to call back and he'd schedule "some tests."

The medication didn't work, and by the end of the second day she was so weak and exhausted that she couldn't even entertain the thought of getting up and going anywhere; and so she suffered through; resting during those times when the torturous symptoms faded; knowing she'd need every ounce of strength and energy, should they come back. And so they did; over and over and over again…

It was the end of the third day; the worst by far; she was beginning to wonder if maybe she should have called 911 and been admitted to the nearest hospital, but something inside – way down deep at the core of her being – made her believe that whatever was happening to her, needed to reach fruition.

She'd lost all concept of time; completely consumed; fading in and out of consciousness; fearing she were about to die; when he came softly; riding the last painful tide.

She recognized him immediately; The Ancient One – her Native spirit guide; the wise one who travels between time; and suddenly all was calm.

She felt the warmth of the fire, whose flames danced in the darkened sky. She smelled the sweet smoke that he cupped in his hands and poured over her weary head. "You have done well my child – now you must rest."

"What's happening to me," she whispered. "Shhh...don't speak...listen" She closed her eyes; falling helplessly into a sublime state of relaxation; concentrating on nothing but the sound of his voice; his words weaving images that filled her completely.

"You have been in the Dark Night of the Soul; a spiritual transformation; one that empties you completely; physically – emotionally – mentally and spiritually; a test of your spirit upon meeting your other half." She stirred restlessly upon hearing the words "other half," but he quickly settled her and continued.

He spoke of Soul Mates and Twin Flames; the difference being that we can have multiple soul mates; those we have many lifetimes and experiences with, who help us grow and evolve; creating and dissipating karma; but as for a Twin Flame, each of us having but one; the soul splitting; each half going their own way; incarnating several times, as they gather human experiences before reuniting in their last lifetime; the release of creative energy, to be used for their spiritual mission; the ultimate goal being that they may ascend together; the twin soul connection; two people connected by soul; connected to God.

"This will be the most fulfilling relationship you can enter into as a human; a rarity not to be taken lightly; more intense than any other union; a love so unconditional, as to be Divine; existing on all levels, but beginning at the level of the soul. There can be nothing between you to block the closeness, when in the presence of your twin."

"How will I know if it's really him?" she asked; his soft laughter lulling her deeper into the infinite abyss. "This meeting will be so life-changing and profound that such a question need not be asked; a union guaranteeing a deeper connection and understanding of Universal Oneness; but make no mistake, my child; the challenge will come in loving unconditionally, without expectation; your longing and desire to be with one another overwhelming; but over time you will come to understand that this longing is to join with the Divine; as two halves of the greater whole." She smiled in quiet contemplation; believing for the first time, in miracles.

"There will be much work, in cleansing your karmic pasts; this task which must be completed together, will bring challenges that force you to grow and heal; mentally, physically and spiritually; while you learn to see beyond your physical limitations, ego, and time itself. Your intense desire will drive you toward one common goal; to be the absolute best manifestation of your spirit on earth; tested by fire – enduring beyond all time and space."

She returned to the material world; forever changed; seeing and experiencing life in a whole new and different way; the possibilities suddenly endless; imagination limitless; her pain and pleasure no longer hers alone; enmeshed and reunited with her one Twin Soul.

And so begins the story of Archibald and Clarissa…

Unconditional

His silence is
Deafening
She knows not
What it
Means

Wandering aimlessly
A beauty in
Desolation
Praying for his
Return

This is his
Truth
She accepts and trusts
Willingly
As patiently she
Waits –

AS IT WAS TOLD

You walked alongside the path enough to recognize it – you jumped on with no hesitation. Why you ask; to be told – taught – shown. You do not walk alone. The key you held unlocking the gate – holding it all along – *we each hold the key* – you said yourself – words guiding – unable to see their meaning; spirit lays in wait – coaxing through the gate – slamming shut as you turn back.

There is no turning back – it's already happened – your fear useless. You gather tools – not knowing why; the need to unload – simplify – rid your self of material possessions that are of no use. Teach the child – hold him close – as you walk the path he clings in spirit – already sensing the parallel.

ALIVE AFTER DYING

Searing heat rising
Consuming from within
Soul awash in flame
Emanating screams of crucifying pain

Tears of despair
Like a river doeth flow
Uninvited intrusion
Like razorblades upon tenderized flesh

Wake to dark silence
No solace no joy
Grasp at dreams fragments
Fleetingly bask in surreal calm

Acting with no reaction
No more have a nice day
Nothing left to lack integrity
Truth that could no longer be denied

Emotionlessly adrift
Perceptions sudden shift
Lost within the illusion
Acceptance in eternal numbness

No more decisions
Refusal to partake in the game
Only the opening to what is the memory of what was
Such is the reality of life after a living death –

INSIDE LOOKING OUT

Tribal winds blow flutes calming melody
Drumbeats surround and penetrate the soul

Ancient One wanders beckoning me forward
Drifting on the horizon a distant illusion

I reach out in vain urgent need to understand
Meaning of his message always in disguise

Carry me away from here take me far away
I beg of thee please release me from this pain

Release you seek at these hands of mine
Reflection mirrored when you explore inside

Unbound the soul of constricting ties
Only then can you truly seek and find

There is no pain of which you speak
Understand this and no more need will there be –

FEEL GOOD MOMENT

They were digging trenches on the grounds that surrounded the complex when I arrived; day laborers, in their orange neon vests with putrid yellow stripes – shovels in hand, tearing up the ground.

I'd been at my desk for about an hour when I saw the orange reflection in the glass coming up the walk. He walked right in with no hesitation, "Excuse me ma'am, would you happen to have a restroom I could use?" A simple enough request; men's room right around the corner, but because of the nature of our business we do not allow it. "I'm sorry, we don't have public restrooms," I said. He gave a little nod, thanked me and left.

As I watched him walk away I felt like shit; and couldn't help but wonder what he'd do now; realizing that the posh ladies room down the hall that I visit 3 or 4 times a day – with plants on the sink, floral scented spray and individual bottles of designer hand soap at each basin is something that I absolutely take for granted. I thought about it for a long time and then forced it from my mind; turning my attention back to spreadsheets and figures; my eyes too blind to see.

Lunch rolled around and I went out on the patio; humidity so thick in the air that I could hear my curls threatening to frizz the moment I walked through the door; but I sat, smoked and suffered; as this is my daily ritual; opting for caffeine, nicotine and a bit of solitude and fresh air, in place of air conditioned kitchen, company of others and food.

I returned to my desk, only to discover a mound of paperwork stacked to the rafters; my immediate response…"Fuck!" and then he walked back through the door, orange vest covered in dirt; haggard and exhausted; dripping sweat from head to toe; looking as if he'd aged 10 years from a mornings worth of back-breaking work. "I'm sorry to bother you again, ma'am, but you wouldn't happen to have a water fountain, would you?" I shook my head, apologized and told him no, but we have soda machines in the kitchen. He thanked me once more and left.

I slumped in my chair, head in hands and let the tears freely flow; not really sure why I was crying, but certain it was such a mix that I wasn't ready to begin picking apart. I sat in silence, staring at my surroundings; leather wingback chairs for impromptu soirees, elegant cabinets to store my files; personal items scattered about; my *'je ne se qua'* as Louis calls it; realizing just how fucking lucky I was.

I grabbed the crispest dollar bill I had from my wallet and made a beeline to the kitchen, inserted it into the machine and grabbed the bottle of water. I left the office and marched my business clad, high heel wearing, Coco Mademoiselle smelling ass down the sidewalk in search of that man; wishing suddenly for my flip flops and jeans, as I passed a dozen or so workers on the way; waist deep in the trenches, all stopping to take a good, long stare; and then I spotted him; all the way out by the road. And so I walked with purpose, on a personal mission; not sure why but nonetheless driven.

"Excuse me, sir?" I yelled from the sidewalk at the edge of the lawn. He didn't hear me, but a strapping young buck did; smiled and then nudged the frail looking older man. He looked up, saw me there and smiled, as he made his way across the grass. His eyes lit up as he approached and I held out the water to him.

"I'm sorry we don't have a water fountain," I said sincerely. He took the water and smiled, "Thank you, angel; bless your heart; bless your sweet heart," he said again and again; our eyes meeting for a brief moment; his showing his true age that his body disguised; who knows what he saw in mine.

As I turned and made my way back to the office, my footsteps felt a little lighter, the sun shone brighter; its rays shifting from nauseatingly hot, to soothing, comforting warmth that filled me from the inside out.

TOO LATE TO DIE YOUNG

It started as a day like any other, but by mid-morning she was so agitated with the people and the world around her that she left work at lunch and didn't go back. Instead she drove home, packed a bag, grabbed her laptop, left a note, said good bye to her dog and hit the road; driving mile after endless mile, not sure where she was going, just following the coast, north on A1A. Thoughts spinning in time with the odometer; none of them complete; snippets of shit weighing on her mind; building for weeks on end; leading her to this place of desolation from which she feared there was no turning back; despair and fury driving her forward to nowhere.

Psychotherapy to fix her troubled mind – thank god it wasn't the 1950's, lest she already be committed; hooked up with high voltage coursing through her brain. A shift in personality, responsibilities askew – *fix her, fix her, make her brand new.* "It's not my personality," she screams; "It's my total perception; why can't you understand?!" Furious at having to defend her self and try to make them understand something that she didn't yet understand herself. A spiritual awakening she claimed and they scoff; wondering if they should contact pastor or priest.

Message on cell phone at ten minutes till five – office closed by the time she calls back – 24 hour wait in which she thought she'd lose her mind. Mammogram results; nodular density compression retest – right breast; what does that mean – can't be sure yet. There must be some mistake; he was with her that day; even made her pray. Your body is perfect – just the way God made it; I promise you're alright; i am the light...I Am the Light...I AM THE LIGHT.

And what of this light which others so freely speak?

A beacon of light others can see by; reminding her that when she sits silently along the rocky shore of life, she is guiding others. Her ship having already come in and now being the time for her to help others navigate along their path. Reminding her that in her solitude, her creative

spirit gives comfort and relief to others; a gift to be shared with those she cares about and people she will never meet.

What happens when the light fades and darkness is all that remains? Who will be there to guide and help *her* navigate along the path? What happens when her spirit loses its creativity and not even she finds comfort and relief in what once brought solace and offered a means of escape? What then...

Perhaps somewhere between the distance of miles the answer will reveal itself. The road beckons and for the first time in her life, she's following the call.

DEEP STILL BLUE

She was young, yet had experienced more life than people she knew thrice her age. She was naïve, in that she tried to see the good in even the wickedest of souls. She never met a person she didn't like, until they gave her reason; and then she was done, just like that.

She came from a town so small that everyone knew her name and thought they knew her business. What they didn't know they made up along the way; never thinking for a moment that she'd become a writer and weave their debauched stories into her own.

Success being her ultimate revenge; poetic license her vengeance.

Along the path she had many men, none of which satisfied, but simply sufficed as entertainment or mere exercise. She loved being a nameless face in a city of millions, but that face was one that would not easily fade into any crowd; as she always stood out above all others, drawing them like bees to nectar. They sought and pursued her; wined and dined her; angered, amused, haunted and stalked her, but never satisfied her; never made her feel the way a woman wants a man to make her feel; and not one of them ever loved her. In truth, they never even knew her.

She believed that was okay, convinced herself that she was the one using them, until one day she woke with eyes wide open and realized that all was not as it appeared to be, and it was not okay. Suddenly the world took on a strange and different hue; the ugliness and evil diffusing the light, causing her own to flicker and fade; eventually learning how to live and maneuver in the dark; even finding comfort in its black embrace.

Twenty years later she woke in the midst of a turbulent storm; not along the shore of which she now dwelled, but deep within the core of her soul. She walked down the hall, turned on the light, gazed at the reflection in the mirror; realizing she'd been dreaming all along.

"Who are you?" she whispered, leaning in closer; watching the smile slowly appear, as finally she heard the answer.

CATCHING FIREFLIES

Electric blue
Trancelike state
Mind connects
Thirst quenched

Giving completely
Fulfilling needs

Doors burned
Truth accepted
Hearts unite
Fear released

Soothing calm
Promises made

To love
To dream
To hope
To be

WILL YOU

Will you still want me
When I'm old and gray
The sparkle in my eyes
All but gone away

Will you support me through
My ups and downs
Just be there to listen
Holding my hand

Will you find the patience
To stay as long as it takes
For me to become what it is
I already think I am

Will you love me forever
As I know I'll love you
Will you wash away these fears
With hours of endless kisses

Will you be by my side
As I take my last breath
Will you promise to keep me
Until the very end –

CLOSER TO FREE

The rains came; and with it, a cool breeze wafted through her window; so strong as to blow the hair from her face; bringing a moments relief from the nights oppressive heat; which sadly matched her mood.

She closed her eyes, leaned her head back and sat in perfect stillness; losing herself in the winds caress; the sound of the gentle soft rain; as if the world were whispering *hush*, instructing her to go deeper; inside her mind, past the pain, to embrace those lingering thoughts.

The harder it fell, the deeper she went; until the walls threatened to close in and consume her. Fleeing captivity she threw open the door, running through the courtyard, a woman lost; half mad; possessed. The cool stones slippery under her feet; her body drenched; her spirit free.

No more what if's and why's of it all; no more lies and self deceit; only the truth of what she knows; who she is, what she feels. There are no deals to be made with the devil, for she tried that pact long ago; life is short, the road is narrow and second chances are few; you can grab it by the balls, or take it by the hand; but in the end, if you let it, regret will surely kill you.

Her hands are on the wheel
Moonlight on her skin
Weight of the world drifting
Taking in all in

She see's the light shining
Just around the bend
She rushes full speed
There's no looking back

She's taken the wheel
She's taking control…

ONE WANT

To be
Enough

As
  I

    Am…

SWAN SONG

She rushes the stage, long after the last curtain call; hoping for one final dramatic and theatrical appearance; playing to an audience of one. One lone soul sitting quietly in the front row, watching the pitiful performance play itself out; for all others have already gone.

As a woman she understands and sympathizes; the loss, the need, the wanting so much to believe. As his woman, she spreads and reads the cards; the deck full of their truth, their oneness, their past, present and future; so tightly bound as to leave no room for uncertainty or doubt.

As a critic she grows bored; the storyline weak, holding no merit, ineffectual and quite frankly lacking in talent and verve. Its time to leave the stage dear – this theatre now closed.

UNCOMFORTABLY NUMB

It started out as an "oh, by the way," and ended in mild confrontation. Her doctor having suggested she start weaning herself from her medication; mothers little helpers that alter the chemicals in her brain and make her happy; even when she's not; a dose taken daily, sometimes twice, for four long, numb years.

Fuck weaning…she quit cold turkey and had been cruising along just fine; focusing and channeling her own energy; aligning her chakras; becoming one with the universe and when necessary, curing her pain with chi-gong. She was pleased with her progress, pleased with her self for taking this step; this monumental step on her path to healing.

"Well, what the hell happens when you have another episode?" he paused only long enough to take a deep breath. "I'll tell you what happens, that's when I call your doctor and tell *him* to deal with you…"

Episode; defined as moments when she becomes a crazy bitch; when the shit gets to be too much and she blows her stack, says what's on her mind, what she thinks, what she feels; even if it's not what people want to hear; fueled by anger, fear, frustration and overall hatred; for being forced to set her dreams aside and play a part in a game prescribed by society; a game in which she no longer wants to be a pawn.

He walked out without another word, she turned and walked to the bathroom, opened the medicine chest, shook out two blue pills, popped them in her mouth and chewed with malicious intent; savoring the painful bite that assaulted her mouth then swallowed without so much as a drop of water; wanting the bitter taste to linger.

She turned off the light, made her way down the hall, climbed in bed, set the alarm and called it another day.

RUNNING IN THE SHADOWS

One more crisis
      Diverted
One more time
      Forced
To face fear
      Alone

CONFESSION

Moments past that seem now so trivial; yet the confession dire that I could have once loved him. Undressed my mind for him; opened my heart to him; bared my soul, embraced his insanity, succumbed to the illusion that he was; and concerned myself deeply with what he thought of me.

LAST TRAIN

Putrid pink walls
Disgusting dirty floor
Running behind schedule
My time too valuable

For this

Her cold hands
On my breast
Pain and discomfort
Stops to examine closely

My tattoos

Four films later
I sit alone
Waiting for radiologist
Whose running way late

Fuck him

I'm so sorry
Ultrasound is necessary
They see something
Need a closer look

My God

Dial his number
Rings and rings
He doesn't answer
I leave no message

Still alone

Just a cyst
No big deal
See you back
Again in six months

Major relief

Oh hell no
You're not waiting
Call your doctor
They can't be sure

Mother freaked

Packing my bags
I'm leaving today
I'm running away
On the next train

Blue train

HIDDEN KEY

He enters the front door
Never through the back
She invited him in
Gave him a key

And so it was different
Right from the start

Permission granted
To delve and explore
The depths of her heart
The halls of her soul

LION TAMER

He waits in silent darkness for to her to come to him; one eye always open, ready to pounce at any given moment. She stealthy steals through the night, avoiding certain areas; sometimes sitting in one place for hours, just so as not to wake him. He alludes to what he wants; she feigns ignorance and hopes he doesn't persist.

The days are less troublesome, for in her confinement of conformity, she finds comfort, even freedom. But the nights grow long and dreary; never knowing what to expect; hiding behind the invisible wall in secret she has built.

He looms in the shadows, a keeper with a stick; prodding through the bars to make his presence known; regain her attention; tame her at whatever cost. The lioness lays weary, exhausted from the fight, seeking only refuge in the still and silent night.

Gathering strength, the lion at her back, waiting for the inevitable moment when finally she strikes back.

UNDONE

The house was empty, but for the child sleeping peacefully down the hall; and so night fell softly at her feet, and she was able at last to settle and find rest within peaceful sleep. Until the witching hour rolled round and brought with it his footfall on the stairs.

He climbed in bed and immediately reached for her; she jumped with a start as if scared half to death. *"I want to have sex,"* he boldly announced; to which she looked at him and laughed; leaving his question, *"what the hell was that"* hanging between them. She rolled over without a word, hugging her pillow tight, as he kissed the back of her neck and vowed to get her in the morning.

And so he did, the minute the first alarm sounded; reaching over and pulling her to him; hands desperately groping her still warm flesh; the weight of his body suddenly pressing down, taking what he believed to rightfully be his. His arousal spurred by selfish greed, as she twisted and writhed beneath him; the words of her friend suddenly ringing in her ears, *"numb, baby, numb..."* and so she became; still and motionless, barely breathing; watching his face as he hovered above, disdain filling her heart, as each penetrating thrust bruised her already wounded soul.

As a smile of satisfaction and accomplishment splayed across his face, she closed her eyes, turned her head to the side, and burned the image forever in her mind. The image of the man who promised to love and cherish, so blinded by his own unrelenting need and skewed vision of the truth that even though she lay beneath him, he had no realization that she'd already left the room.

She was no longer viewed as a person; with feelings, wants and needs of her own, but simply a possession, a plaything, a caretaker, a maid;

and as she lay alone, bathed in dawns light, not wanting to be any of those things, a single tear fell from her eye, as she made a silent vow.

ONE UGLY TRUTH

He didn't want to go. He made that fact perfectly clear; said he was only doing it for her and she'd owe him big time. She would have happily gone without him, it wasn't as if she needed an escort, but simply preferred it; wanted him to share in this experience; if for no other reason, a bit of culture would do him good; because while he was a fine piece of eye-candy, he had absolutely nothing else going for him.

He could be rather dashing when he wanted to, and although she loved the way he looked in his tuxedo and bowtie, the smells from The Gentlemen's Club he carried home with him each night made her sick to her stomach. She only hoped he'd take the time to stop by the apartment and change before he met her at Music Hall.

Not only did he not bother to change, but apparently hadn't been working late at all, as he showed up drunk; calling her name as he staggered down the center isle during act II of The Mask of Orpheus; just as Orpheus was about to hang himself. Her heart sank in her chest, as everyone turned to look at the beautiful, pitiful creature, and she was forced to leave her seat, claim him and remove him from the theatre.

Later that night he lay passed out on the bed, as she sat in the corner and watched him; loathing and contempt building with each breath he took, as this truly was the last straw. She never knew what it was to hate, until she came to know the likes of him, and why the fuck she married him was beyond her even then.

As the hours passed and the moon rose over the river, its shadows mingled with the lights of the city and shined through the window, she knew she had to get rid of him; and sending him packing just wouldn't do. She'd tried to tell him it was over, that their marriage was a sham, but he was like stray dog; once fed he just kept coming back. No…she'd reached the point with only one option left.

She thought about poisoning him, but what if he survived; as his wife she'd be stuck caring for him the rest of her life. She knew a man on Third and Vine; a seedy sort that caught her eye, as she was passing the square late one afternoon. They became fast friends and occasional lovers; and while he made for an interesting romp, the nipple clamps and bondage just really wasn't her style.

However, while discussing her predicament one night over sushi and Saki, he mentioned a connection. For a mere five grand he could leave for work on any given day, never to be seen or heard from again. She thought about it for a minute, calculating her budget and determining how soon she could come up with the cash, but the thought of him being tortured in an old abandoned warehouse in the industrial district, his pretty face pummeled to mush, ruined her appetite.

So there she sat, contemplating his demise, when her gaze shifted to the lamp that sat on the bedside table, weighing every bit of forty pounds. Suppose he tried to get out of bed and stumbled; the lamp crashing down on his head. No, that would never do, as the distance the lamp had to fall between the table and the bed, couldn't possibly land a fatal blow. But one to the side of his head, right on the temple would do the trick, no doubt; she immediately thought of the hammer she kept in the kitchen drawer.

But then she'd have to get rid of the body; and while they lived in a high rise along the river, she'd never be able to drag him to the waters edge by herself; not without being seen, and suppose he just floated there and didn't sink. Better still, she could lure him out on the balcony and in one felled swoop…over the rail, a twelve story drop…YES…that would surely do!

In the end she didn't do any of those things, because as much as she hated him, she didn't really want him dead, she just wanted him gone.

She fell asleep in the chair and woke when the sun rose and immediately began gathering his things; two duffle bags, his guitar in its case and a one-way ticket to Connecticut sat in the alcove just outside the door. She'd taken his keys and as soon as he dragged his sorry ass out of bed, asked if he'd go down the corner store for coffee, as she'd forgotten to pick it up the day before.

He got dressed, left the apartment and let out a loud "what the fuck," when he realized what was happening. The door locked automatically once it was closed, and just as he turned and reached for the knob, he heard the bolt securing it further.

She apologized to her neighbors and the security guard, for their Sunday morning had been ruined, but she never apologized to him, for only she knew just how close he came to not walking away at all.

IMAGINE

Closing your eyes
Flying away
Without a thought or care
Embracing the truth
Releasing all pain
No penalty
No price
To pay –

SEA BREEZE

The waves break softly
Upon the shore
Low tide rising
Sand bar dark blue
Beneath a turquoise
Sea

It laps coolly
At her feet
Her ankles
Her waist
Her breasts
Her neck

Suddenly in
Over her head

Submerged...

Feeling the power
Ebb and flow
Washing away demons
Cleansing her soul

Baptismal font of the
Universe
Strips away all
Leaves behind only
Truth

Her truth
The one that sets
Her free
The one nobody wants
To see

She breaks the
Surface
Face raised toward
The sun
Takes one final
Breath
They say she's
Come undone

Back under she
Goes
Relaxed…relieved
Devoid of all
Pain
Undertow carries her
Away

The hum of the
Miles
The distance
Between
Into oblivion
Gone with the
Breeze –

I AM

My words fail me
I am empty

Darkness falls
I am alone

The world suffocates
I am unhappy

The storm rages
I am weary

Tomorrow is unknown
I am hopeful

AT WORLDS END

Sunrise on the ocean
Bringing peace and calm
Hours of sanctity
Spent before the dawn

Heaven on earth
Fringing the illusion
Picture window offering
Front row view

To be
Like this
Forever

VISIONS OF CHANGE

She stood like a rock, against the raging storm; and although there were those that looked on from afar; they never knew how she was torn. For this storm was different and of monumental proportion; leaving her mentally worn and emotionally ravaged. But as with all storms, the calm soon came; followed by two days of peaceful bliss; upon which she cast all her faith.

The voice of truth spoke and so she did listen; silently taking in each and every detail. Forced to purge outdated and misused information; stored randomly and without plausible cause; just there to simply fill up the files. And so purge she did; emptying those files with reckless abandon; making way for the new, the absolute; what she always believed, now confirmed as pure truth.

Two glorious days upon which the foundation was cemented and sealed; ideals and beliefs no longer out of reach; not to mention that of dreams.

And then came the inevitable; the moment she was forced back into the world. Surrounded by gluttonous pigs; plates overflowing with leftovers pushed aside, no thought given to the waste, as they hastily made their way back to the buffet; the buffet of life, filled with inconsequential chatter; casting a strain on her very existence, making her ears bleed until she wanted to scream. Tears falling like rain under the strain; realizing she can no longer pretend or play the game.

For the white view she has seen and suddenly nothing else matters...

T R A C E S

Nothing quite
As clean as
It seems

No…

Not ever

WITHIN WITHOUT

He stood in the doorway, taking in the scene before him; a haunting melody seemingly echoed from nowhere, as the candles cast flickering shadows upon the walls; black tapers in polished brass holders; always black and brass. The smell of incense filling his senses, yet he could not tell from which direction it burned; swirls of invisible smoke wafting; permeating the room.

A room divided by a sheer white veil that hung from the ceiling and fanned out over the floor; the bed clearly visible, illuminated from behind; black satin sheets made for a welcoming sight. He closed the door silently and slowly stepped inside; casting his eyes upon her in the corner, when he heard a muffled cry.

A shard of etched crystal reflecting a flame; the goblet from which she always drank, broken in perfect pieces before him on the floor; a puzzle with one piece missing; the one she now held in her hand; examining closely before the flame.

He spoke but she did not answer; what game was this she was playing. He walked across the room, pushing the veil aside; she turned her attention from the glass and met his gaze with unseeing eyes. "What are you doing," he asked, as he slowly inched closer; she shook her head and he could see that she was crying. He knelt down before her, in her white satin robe; before he could stop her or even realize what she was doing, she cut with intent, one more time; crying out in agonizing pain.

Pain so deep that the slashes on her flesh meant nothing; a means to remind herself she was still alive, fleeting at best, yet unable to surmise; for darkness had crept in and settled upon her soul; and although she was clearly pleading for help, he was too wrapped in himself to recognize what it meant; she didn't want him to save her, she just wanted to die.

He stood and loomed over her; a look of disgust splayed over his face, as her insanity had become way too intense; and so without a word, or a second glance in her direction, he turned and left, never to return.

The next one was different, her ticket to ride; through the portal of illusion into the afterlife. She knew when she walked in and saw the picture over his bed; a Goth chick with strings, attached to her ankles and wrists; the puppet master non other, than the Grim Reaper himself.

She knew he would take her there, she hadn't a doubt; as they raced full throttle from city to town; always under the cover of darkness, as she could no longer tolerate the light. They came close more than once, but fell short every time; in the end the only one he destroyed was him self.

She drifted aimlessly from north to south; touching the lives of all those she encountered; in love or in hate; differing only in disguise. Compromising her self for beliefs and tradition; while trying to maintain some semblance of self; looking for the path to freedom, stumbling each time she believed she'd found redemption.

Then one dark and stormy night, the knock fell upon her door; knowing who stood on the other side before even opening it; she did not hesitate, but flung it open wide; inviting him in to sit for a while.

Beside the fire, fueled by love and understanding, their stories unfolded as if all part of a dream. "Take my hand and walk this way, I've seen the dawn of enlightenment; seek shelter with me along the path, against the illusion of life, we are forced to fight."

His invitation tempting, filled her with hope, but she'd come to the end with no fight left within; she spoke with her eyes as she reached for his hand; he felt the cold steel and understood her master plan.

He did it out of love, because he knew her true soul; although he wanted desperately to walk with her, he understood that she was done. Giving reverence where others had miserably failed, he released her from the bonds of her torturous hell.

He built the pyre and stayed by her side; standing before her with truth in his eyes. He kissed her lips one last time, struck the match and alighted the flame. The road beckoned and the rains finally came, he spoke one final goodbye and went his own way…

In Solitude

The sun sets golden in a clear blue sky; but for the few white plumes lending their signature to the conclusion of this day.

Bucks bistro table for two; occupied by one. Don't Stop the Dance with its sensual sax; caressing my ears, filling my senses; editing of manuscript having reached the end.

Words which instill fear yet bring enormous comfort; having become so familiar in their reading and their meaning; knowing what publication will eventually bring. Left behind; moved beyond; entrusted to my care.

Nietzsche in my bag; portable *and* basic writings; a grounding connection through time and space; *"every philosophy also conceals a philosophy; every opinion a hideout; every word also a mask."*

How well we dwell and dance behind those pretty masks; identities hidden as we interpret life's poem; basic need and want mirrored; revealed only to each other…

"Truth is all that matters; drifting through a world tattered and torn. Love is stormy weather; beauty should be deeper than the skin. Footsteps in the dark come together;
Don't stop…don't stop the dance —

FADE TO BLACK

Darkness falls and for a moment all is calm; waves lap gently upon the shore as silence settles over a tranquil sea. The same moon, the same stars, viewed as one, but from afar; she raises her face to the night, slips quietly away inside her mind. Into those arms she dreamed of and yearned for, where truth and love embraced her; warmed by his light, his touch of purpose, beyond all expectations.

In her loneliness her heart does ache, for she has come to know their purpose. In her heart she holds onto hope, waiting for the moment they unite once more. Into wanting arms she will fall yet again, there will be no turning back; until then she struggles with the truth of the world and in her exhaustion fades to black...

MINDLESS RAMBLE

He was a nasty slob; my immediate thought, superiority complex; drinking coffee from a Styrofoam cup; too cheap to shell out six bucks at Bucks, so he drank gas station rot gut, bought on the fly. Cell phone to his ear, held by fat stubby fingers; obviously berating someone by his facial expressions and the vein on the side of his head that looked as if were about to explode; probably his 19 year old stripper wife.

And there he sat; faded yellow Polo, fat ass squeezed into a super sweet tricked-out Porsche Carrera GT; 440 G's out the door; mother fuck! What's up with ugly guys and bitchin cars?!

He came flying up on my ass and then jetted around and passed, slowing down long enough to take a good long look in my window (as if I should be impressed…as fucking if!) before attempting a Batman move, zig zagging his way through rush hour traffic on San Jose…not happening dude…no matter what kind of ride you drive!

It wasn't 30 seconds after he passed, I saw it coming and put my foot on the brake; a little blue buzz bomb flying across three lanes from the right, as the Porsche was gunning it on the left, both trying to beat the light that was about to turn red. And then…WHAM! The two came together and enmeshed; skidding in a frenzied, out-of-control dance;

bringing four other cars into the mix; blocking all three lanes for the next hour and a half; all because they were driving with their heads up their ass.

And so I sat there in my little van; nothing glamorous, but she's all mine and gets me where I want to go; watching those involved pacing back and forth, each one on the phone making call after endless call. I put her in park and lit up a smoke, my quad shot white mocha still extra hot; and I watched as I waited; my routine put on indefinite hold.

And I couldn't help but think; how something so beautiful could be completely destroyed in a matter of seconds. Thinking about the Porsche of course; which suddenly became a high dollar metaphor for life. In the blink of an eye things come and go; turn the corner and just be gone; everyone in such a fucking rush. Where the hell they all going so fast? What greatness lay in wait at their desired destination that they haphazardly jeopardize so many lives?

What fools these mortals be…

And then I thought of Rocky; Rocky Durosso; his being the first waterfront mansion I visited upon my move to Florida. Rocky was a business owner; Italian, handsome to the bone, wealthy and generous; a wonderful host who opened his home and welcomed me in with open arms; a Benz, Alfa Romeo and Bugatti in the drive, with a house full of rednecks and strippers trashing the place from bottom to top, while he obliviously grilled lobster and marinated scallops on the lawn; making sure everyone's drink remained full, happy with himself for providing such a great time. After all, it was only money; nothing that couldn't be repaired or replaced. Just stuff, meaningless really.

I'd like to think I got it, but I'm not really sure if I did. I just couldn't understand why he surrounded himself with such lowlife dregs, when he seemed to have so much on the ball. He reminded me of Elvis, the way he threw his money around senselessly, in an attempt to buy lovers and friends; keeping people close and happy, but to what end.

The stripper he was fucking got pregnant and then bailed after the kid was born and he refused to marry her. He raised that little girl all by himself. I'd often see them out at dinner, the little princess and her dad. I'd heard the mother died of an overdose, everyone said it was just as well. He seemed to have gotten his shit together and although I didn't know him well, for some reason it made me glad.

Then a few years later, at the age of 56, they found him dead at the Waterfront Omni Hotel; the five star that sits along the banks of the St. Johns in downtown Jacksonville. No drugs, no sign of foul play, just checked into the hotel alone, went to bed and never woke up.

Strange how that works, isn't it?

JUST FUCKED

It was the same back then; the same, only different. Any variation beyond the realm of ordinary routine questioned; frowned upon. My time spent writing, alone inside my mind; misunderstood, misconstrued, becoming a sudden threat; when it had nothing whatsoever to do with them.

The reading of a book, a waste of precious time ; lost in fantasy, what does that say about your life; no thought given to the possibility of expanding knowledge; hadn't a clue as to what the fuck I was reading.

Every move suddenly guarded and gauged; as if a prisoner in the yard on constant display. ***Shakin the bush boss...shakin the bush!***

God forbid should I wake in the night and leave the room; a shadow on my trail questioning what I'm doing. It's beyond stifling, way past nauseating, reaching the point of full blown obsession; terrifying if I stop long enough and really think about it.

What is this inability to let me be; grow; find myself; even if that means walking away. If you love something set it free. That saying on a plaque hung on my wall from the time I could read until the words simply faded away; but what it neglected to say was that it was never yours in the first place; people cannot be owned.

What's so hard about letting me go...

Even when the relationship is in obvious decline, still that need to smother and cling; suddenly shifts into overdrive; to the point where they'd actually lock me away; in a bathroom for two days or an asylum indefinitely; the moment I pack my bags and start for the door.

FUCK ME! I have nothing left to give.

Then I step back and see it for what it really is; thank god I have that ability left within. An ego bruised, chauvinistic pride; because I cheated *with* you and you made me your wife; then I cheated *on* you and ruined your life.

He stands over me now wanting an explanation for my strange behavior. It's after midnight, I cannot sleep; I'm writing, what more is there to tell. It's who I am; it's what I fucking do…remember?!

He shakes his head and retreats from the room; my heart grows heavy with impending doom. Right this moment I wish for daybreak, no comfort will I find in darkness this night, for I know not what awaits me. But in the morn I will rise, shower and change, punch the clock and be free for the day.

THINKING LBEAN

Alfresco at Bucks
White mocha extra whip
Music so loud
I can't fucking think

Sun setting pink
In the western sky
Fame is but a fruit tree
Gotta love Mr. Nick

The Idiot
Sons and Lovers
The Gambler
Big Sur

Sun Also Rises
And Naked Lunch
Visited B&N
Went a little nuts

For a good reason
Checking off the list
Countdown to forever
To pass the time quick

DOWNWARD SPIRAL

Witnessing his spiritual pain
She wonders if she can save him
Through loving and supporting him
Will it ever be enough

When the world is so cruel
And he suffers from its touch
She'll succeed or die trying
Either way she'll give everything

Because she believes
Because she knows
Loves him madly
With her whole heart and soul

From the place of desolation
In which he now dwells
The truth of his spirit
Shining brighter than he knows

QUOTE OF THE DAY

"You can't demand respect from others,
when you haven't an ounce of respect for yourself."

SO TIRED

I'm tired too
Bleeding again and in pain
Why do we fucking bother
I ask myself every day

I could fly to you
Make the trek
Dive off the mountain
Together

Poof...

No
More
Pain

Or just maybe
We'd find something
Worth living for
Along the way

THE TIME IS NOW

Forever looking
Outside her self
Approval
Support
Direction
Rather than looking
Within

Prepared is she
To provide her self
Whatever means
To awaken and unfurl
Her inner being

To stand alone
Face the one
She's always been aware
Never taking time
To become properly
Acquainted

Ready at last
To find what it
Means
To live life for
Her self

Following the call
Her own soul
Refusing to be
Beholden
The expectations
Of others

Seeing the dream
Clearly now
Just that
A dream
Life an illusion
Wearing many
Disguises

GREEN ABYSS

…and then there are days when she doesn't hear from him at all; navigating alone in her world of darkness. She buries herself in her work; #2 on the placebo list, dulling her pain of existence. She works with a vengeance, not pacing herself; running out of diversions; her mind begins to wander, as time ticks slowly by; endless uncertainty, forced to face her fears, the reflection in the mirror; gazing into the green abyss, lost within her own eyes; seeing her self perhaps for the very first time; never before feeling more awake or alive; as others watch from afar, judge and criticize; the last thing she needs; the opinions of those who stare out the window, content to watch as life passes by…

JUST NUMB

I walked in the office and she was crying. I didn't have to ask what was wrong; it was clear, her mother had just died. Her husband was there picking her up, had called and given her the news over the phone; cowardice son of a bitch. She saw me, walked toward me, I opened my arms and she fell into them. I held her close, hugged her to me, without a word, without a single expression of sorrow, with no feeling inside whatsoever; and I wondered what kind of person I was becoming...

SOLITARY WIND

Will I ever
Find
My way
Again…

BESEECH

Wicked wind howls an ethereal lonesome moan
Branches sway wildly under stress a tremored groan
River rises white caps lash violently toward the shore
Rain slashes monstrous claws upon her battered door

Cowering in the corner lights flicker silent fear
Trapped within confinement those walls do draw so near
Every move and thought un-spoke from afar observed
Unseen eyes do constant watch to glimpse of her unknown

Strain of life lived in lies marks deep her tattered soul
Truth unveiled but was not heard conveniently ignored
Step outside and take her place within the wrathful storm
Insanity breaks as thunder cracks lost in labyrinths pain

EPITAPH

She spent endless hours among the dead, tiptoeing around their graves. The moment she passed through the tall iron gates; branches canopying the narrow path, her soul awash in unexplained peace. For here they could not judge, had crossed to the other side, where truth and knowledge lay in wait; the place she so longed to be; searching for traces that might allow her to see.

In her quest for understanding of life and death, she consulted her pastor and scoured endless shelves, absorbing every book she could lay her hands on; coming away disappointed each time; in the realization that there was no secret to be revealed.

Men of the cloth and scholars alike, devoting their entire lives, and while they were versed in religious histories, speculation disguised as fact, in truth they knew no more than her; because the answers can only be found by searching within.

Not human beings who from time to time have a spiritual experience; but spiritual beings having a temporary human experience…that is our truth…that is what we are.

She realized this on a cold November day; walking under a gray sky in the misting rain. She came to a tomb marked King and a chill crept up her spine; it was her great grandfather whom she had never met. She stood and read the epitaph of this man from whose life she sprang and it all became clear.

Loving Father – Faithful Husband – Devout Christian – Worked hard his whole life; an entire life summarized and reduced, to eleven words carved in stone; her heart screamed NO, as there had to be more! And that's when she began looking around, taking notice of the markers she'd been lingered among; each one different, every one the same; human error for this mistake she blamed.

Row after row she wound her way through, frantic now to find one knowing soul; hours spent, soaking wet, with a heavy heart and wavering faith; how could she possibly be right and the rest of the world wrong?

She'd lost all hope, given up; exhausted she made her way back toward the path and just as she was about to step on, a red bird flew so close she could hear the fluttering of its wings; she turned and watched as is alighted on a small, inconspicuous stone, and found the answer she'd been searching for…

Jonathan Marsh
1911 – 1963
"Enjoyed his Human Experience by Living a Free Spirit."

OPEN DOOR

The light of
Day
Is not yet
Seen
I felt him
Earlier
He haunted my
Dreams

He touched me
Softly
He whispered sweet
Words
It's been too
Long
His voice was
Heard

Yet I felt
Him
As many times
Before
He entered
Quietly
Through my minds
Door

FOR A MOMENT

For a moment
Let me be
The one
Who tells you
Stories

Let me be
The one
You lay beside
And rest
With

Just lay down
Beside me
If only
For a
Moment

UNCONDITIONAL

Bring me your darkness
I will cast the light

Bring me your insanity
I will show you good reason

Bring me your dread
I will ease your fear

Bring me your apathy
I will stir your emotions

Bring me the pieces of your shattered soul
I will bond them together to form it whole

Bring me your burdens
I will love you all the more

ON YOUR JOURNEY

Hold on to what is good even if it is a handful of earth. Hold on to what you believe even if it is a tree which stands by itself. Hold on to what you must do even if it is a long way from here. Hold on to life even when it is easier letting go. Hold on to my hand even when I have gone away from you.
~ Pueblo Blessing ~

Know that I believe in you
Know that I have faith in you
Know that I trust in you completely
Know that I am with you every step of the way
Know that I love you now
Know that I always will

QUEST

A single grain of sand, blowing on that white St. Augustine beach; searching for some semblance of peace in her life. A single leaf quivering, among the lush Amazonian trees; on a quest for peace and balance within his own mind.

Simultaneously searching; together – yet separate – to meet again someday at one sudden goal; and blend they then, into one beautiful and perfect whole. And life's endless night will no longer seem so dark; with another knowing soul traversing by their side.

SHEER WEIGHT

Fear is something
We should not feel
To be set free
From the cage of steel

When the soul
Is set soaring
To endless heights
Of infinity

The other side
The unknown world
All we must do
Walk through the door

The blinding light
The piercing screams
None of it real
It's all just a dream

The veil so thin now
As to be transparent
Time to wake up
Stop feeling the pain

Nothing but stardust
Blown to the wind
The solitary wind
The wind of change

LONGING

O northeasterly wind, when whilst thou blow
That the blustering rain can dissolve this pain
Dear God, if my love were in my arms
And I in his bed once more

UNVEILED TRUTH

What can be said
This illusion of
Love

His words still
Haunt her
I love you
But

CHILDHOOD PLAYGROUND

There was a large church that sat on the corner across the street from her house. She used to go there when things got too spooky at home; seeing them watching from the second-story window, trying not to look, but feeling their eyes on her all the same; knowing she was safe and they couldn't touch her, so long as she was across the street at God's house. For hours she'd play on those front steps; up one side, across the landing and down the other.

Then one day she heard a strange noise coming from inside; frozen in fear as the large double doors slowly opened; and there the old lady stood; white hair pulled back in a bun, a kind smile and green eyes that were the color of her own. That was the day she first met Bessie and Jake; their job it was to clean the church. From that day on she had free reign on cleaning days; looking over her shoulder as she made her way inside; wondering what they thought – the dark ones, always watching from the upstairs window.

They were a quiet couple that lived in a little blue house two blocks from her own. She liked being able to be with them in silence; no pressure to perform, speak, or even think for that matter. Usually in the kitchen is where she'd find them; after having slipped through the garden gate; the door hidden among the overgrown honeysuckle that had taken over the fence that surrounded their entire yard. A secret garden in which she could explore and play; without hindrance, without interruption; all alone with her girlish dreams and fantasies.

Through the kitchen door she'd slip; Bessie at the sink in her pretty flowered apron that tied behind her neck and covered her whole dress; washing vegetables or cutting fruit that she'd gathered from the garden; allowing her to eat them straight from the bowl. Jake at the table with his little leather pouch and funny looking machine; she always enjoyed watching him measure out the precise amount and then roll the perfect cigarette; the sweet smelling tobacco filling the room.

Content she was, just to be in their presence; Bessie and Jake, her great-grandparents, who she discovered quite by mistake. Hers was a strange upbringing to say the least; for even though the little blue house had sat empty and abandoned, several years even before she was born; the dead had a way of showing themselves, never remaining so; not in her world, where the veil blew freely between worlds, as if controlled by the breeze...

A W A K E N I N G

With his words he touched her soul
Breathed all that was real
Into her world

Her eyes were opened
And she thought to herself

Yes…

This is the way it was intended –

STONE OF THE SKY

We sat before the fire; flames sparking blue powerful magic. The vast sky a black velvety canvas; sprinkled with billions of pinpoints of light. The sweet pungent smoke making me dizzy in my altered state of consciousness. Off to the side he lay; naked upon a buffalo robe; a vision of beauty and peace. The Ancient One walking around him, in slow deliberate circles; blowing smoke, casting herbs, chanting to the spirits to send clear guidance.

The Ancient One stopped; I could see the light connecting them; pale blue, flickering in intensity, as he knelt beside him, his hand open wide, hovering just above his chest. Eyes closed, face raised toward the heavens, he took a deep breath, as if inhaling his essence, then began to speak…

"He holds powerful energy – breaking through the grip of limitations and constraints – stirring within the womb, hidden beneath the surface."

He remained as he was and said, "This one you love…" not a question, more than just a statement. I said, "Yes," and watched as his hand moved slowly upward, lingering now above his head.

"His power of thought precedes manifestation – mental activity ruling his life; constant motion weakens him – but he bends with the wind, adapting with persistence. His life path lit by the light of hope; but another, more fragile light as well; one that is long lasting and that of the stars. It is the light that reveals separation as illusion, and the oneness of existence. He holds truth that the spiritual sky and physical earth are interwoven; this is the light that leads him."

"This one is a traveler – following a guiding vision of the future; growing out of struggles, disappointments and pain of the past and present. His faith is the assurance of things to come. His clarity takes him with exhilaration in all directions. His desire is wisdom – knowing why – putting that knowledge to work."

He stood and walked toward me, taking my hand, lifting me up so that I stood before him. The truth and assuredness seen in his eyes, like nothing I've ever known.

"You must bring him the stone of the sky – of the mystical realm; to enhance his understanding, clear his energy pattern; brining him calm and peace – good balance and energies. A dreamer, a visionary, of this vitality is vulnerable to emotional disturbance; when blocked he will withdrawal; disorder causing physical, mental and emotional discomfort. Help him establish direction and there he will find fulfillment."

"Always with the stone…the stone of the sky."

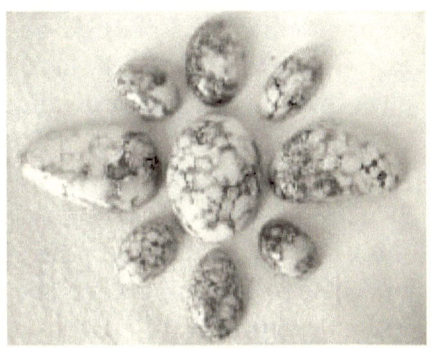

DIVINE RETRIBUTION

I'll never forget the day I found the guitar case buried in the back of his closet; my heart falling to pieces next to it on the floor. Letters and cards dated from just weeks before; how good he felt inside her, how she couldn't wait to have her lips on him again. She mentioned me by name, though I was too blinded with rage to recognize the jealousy.

The penmanship atrocious, too many grammatical errors to even count; and Polaroid's of her skanky ass posed beside her Monte Carlo; two of her on the circa 1960 couch, breasts peeking out of the cheap polyester blouse; with that come fuck me look on her face.

I sat for hours, reading until my eyes blurred; memorizing her features until my stomach turned. Gazing at my own reflection in the mirror; as different as day and night; wondering what he saw in that white-trash blonde; deducing finally that because of the age difference, it must have been the sex.

I was young, inexperienced, a virgin when we met; so what competition could I possibly be, to someone so much older and more experienced; even though there was nothing he wanted that I didn't give; I was a good girl, plain and simple; when obviously he wanted a whore.

I came across her a year or so ago, on one of my trips passing through; she recognized me immediately, though it took me a moment or two. I smiled and placed my order, she turned her gaze away; I persisted, she had no escape; forced finally to look at me. I asked for lemon on the side then inquired as to her name; to which she responded, Dianna, through all five rotten teeth.

MISFIT

.....and if I close my eyes and drift away, where would my thoughts take me. For at times it feels there is nowhere left to go; all my minds doors closed and locked tight; and if forced to venture outside my own realm; reality strikes that I simply don't fit.

S U S T E N A N C E

His words of want
Sustain me
Make me feel
Alive

Touching some place
Inside of me
I believed
Had long since
Died

CONFUSION HAS ITS COST

Grasping the illusion nothing is nothing
Stranded in fear pain feels so real

Inner world of spiritual being
Outer world of flesh and blood

Remove him from the picture
Both worlds appear undeveloped

Confusing paths and purpose
Loves consuming delusion

Momentary lapse in reason
Feel her self coming undone

Slips slowly into waiting comfort
Dark abyss once more embraced

REFLECTION

I saw contempt
I saw grace
I saw madness
I saw angst

I saw passion
I saw emptiness
I saw immorality
I saw forgiveness

I saw fury
I saw mercy
I saw greed
I saw kindness

I saw love
I saw hate
I saw life
I saw death

As I gazed at my
Reflection
In the rearview
Mirror

UNRESTRAINED

I never asked
That he
Need me
I only want
That he should
Love me

His path shrouded
In shadowy
Darkness
Torturous thoughts
Render him
Helpless

I'll endure such
Demons
Ruling that
Realm
Brazenly searching
His deepest
Desires

SPIRIT OF FEAR

My darkness is such
That I cannot breathe
Suffocating slowly
This void of
Emptiness

Tired of the world
In which I dwell
Held hostage by
Wicked demon
Spells

Oh, to end this
Lingering misery
Say your goodbyes
Kiss me twice

Shove me in quickly
A commonplace causality
Drowning in the angst filled
Well of our lives

In Dreams

He rose from the depths of her unconscious mind, like smoke drifting from the unknown; wrapping himself around; penetrating her soul.

"I feel you...I feel you," she whispered softly; as dawns light crept in and slowly he faded into morning's mist; just as she reached out to bring him to her.

ONE OF THOSE MOMENTS

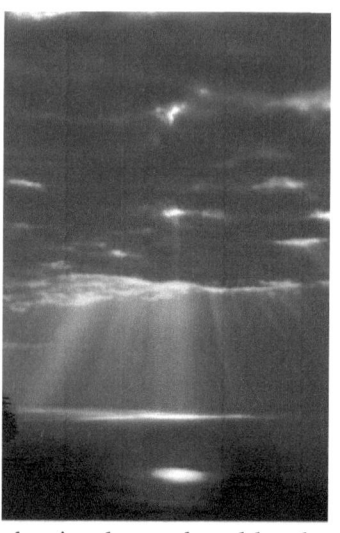

It was one of those moments when you know for certain something more than our imaginations are capable of fathoming, lingers just beyond the veil of illusion; a vision of hope, meant possibly and seen perhaps, only by me.

It was early morning; the sky was filled with ominous, rapid-moving clouds; the grey reflecting my mood, my pain, the storm that had become my life; trying to wrap my head around and distinguish truth from lies; wondering how I'd get through the day; would I ever again find my way; having been slayed by those wrathful demons, or rather that one ruling beast; trying to rationalize the reasoning; my worth as a person, my talent as a writer; both suddenly seeming minor at best.

I stopped where I was, turned up the volume and let the soothing sounds of Botti's Italia caress my soul, ease my mind, recognize my pain. Caruso was playing when I finally opened my eyes; a break in the sky, a black jagged hole, fringed with frilly white; a single sunbeam breaking through, fanning light among the dark.

The hole in the sky reflecting the one in my soul; surrounded by darkness, filled with a single ray of hope.

LESSON 18

I am not alone in experiencing the effects of my seeing
I am not alone in experiencing the effects
I am not alone in experiencing
I am not alone
I am not
I am

alone

TORMENTED MIND

His life is a bittersweet symphony
Refusing to slave for money
Drifting through life
Waiting to die

All the roads he's been down
Lead to the exact same place
Voices in his head
Screaming for release

Haven't prayed in years
Tonight I'm on my knees
Protect him in his aloneness
Allow him a moments peace

FORGETTABLE

His truth was brutal, and while she hated him for the things he did and
the pain he inflicted, still, she was left wondering of her own character
and what caused him to see her as one so easily manipulated,
dismissed and forgettable.

S H E

She is the big sister I never had but always wanted; who speaks her mind and isn't afraid to be her self, no matter how different her views or what anyone thinks; just like me.

She is the timid writer, afraid to hit the publish button each time she puts her thoughts into words, for fear of what any and all who read will think; just as I once was.

She is lonely and lovely, looking for love; unconditional, can't live without each other love; just as I once looked.

She is intelligent and strong willed; with beliefs and virtues that don't fit inside any mold; a woman of the world, her own world; just the way she likes it; just like I do.

She is a woman with one missing piece to her puzzle; believing beyond all doubt that the twin flame of her soul burns bright in some distant night sky; searching as I was.

She questions what she's been taught of religion; believing in a higher power, just not certain it resembles that which has been written; aware of her own powers, yielding them wisely; as I have done for years.

She is talented and worthy, having claimed some semblance of victory; over the trials and tribulations this life has to offer; suffering and overcoming, growing wiser and stronger for each passing experience, refusing to be beat; as I have and continue to do.

She has been called to the table to play the game; dealt a card by the master hand of wicked games; claiming to have been led by destiny, testing her faith, skewing her perception, telling his stories that warrant pity, taking every scrap she's willing to give, then leaving her filled with self loathing and doubt; the chair still warm from where I once sat.

He claims to have found the last; destroyed and evened the score; but he is a deceitful liar, hell-bent on atonement and will continue to prey on unsuspecting victims; looking for the link that ties them each together.

Take heed…

If you come upon him one night, knocking at your door, plying you with soulful words; claiming a connection, never wanting to label you, only wanting to love you; seeming heaven-sent, too good to be true; run like hell, for the demon wears many disguises, playing upon every emotion; but make no mistake, he goes straight for the soul….

A L O N E

Her last glimpse of the world
Her last breath drawn
Her last tear shed
Her final moment of fear

Spent alone

The way
She lived
Her life

To
The
End…

VILLAINS & VICTIMS

So as I was pondering the bittersweet symphony of his life on my way to work this morning, I couldn't help but wonder; in his mind, exactly what constitutes a friend and where within I would fall asunder. Now while I realize this was a total waste of energy and time, because in the end it makes no difference whatsoever, but still, that's me; always wondering, adding unneeded stress.

While I have an extra bed upon which he could rest, never will he lay there. While I have a life I believed he wanted to share, never will he be a part of. And while I have knowledge of the industry in which he needs to sell his craft, I've shared that knowledge, did what I could do, and watched him walk away still; a victim of his own fear, running from calamity, or simply making excuses to justify his abhorrent behavior?

Wondering now, where that leaves me and exactly what I am a victim of; ego-driven self indulgence perhaps...

US – THEM

His world is small
Her world is too large
He barely leaves his room
She is forced to leave hers daily

He can move in his world
She is confined and constricted
He doesn't want to
It's all she dreams of

Too hard for him to decide
She knows exactly
Which way to go
Wherever he is

The silence rips his mind
In silence she finds peace
The solitude tears his soul
The solitude tears hers too

A singular abyss
Sounding the depths
Darkness sings to it all
Sweet melody of Stygian

His world his small
Is there room enough for two

IN DIVINE DUALITY

They broke
Him
Collectively
As he broke
Them
Individually

INFINITE ENCOUNTER

Many choose to forget what they don't want to remember. I will always remember, never let myself forget; so as to better be armed the next time around; I find myself lost on that darkened path; the passageway leading to his domain, where shadows and illusion will find us again —

SEEMINGLY BREATHING

"Did you really want to kill yourself, baby?"

There was a long pause of silence, in which her mind tried to decide; truth or lie. He waited in anticipation; reaching in, feeling her pain; she whispered, *"Yes,"* he closed his eyes.

"Fuuuck," the word long - drawn out - soft on his breath, running his fingers through his hair. *"I promise I'll never leave you; I've burned that door forever; just you and me baby, sooner then later."*

Her pain was real, as she struggled to survive in the dark abyss. She stared too long into it and found him looking back at her.

THEREIN LIES

The truth…

There is no truth nor are there any lies; only our own personal interpretations of how we perceive ourselves and the world around us. It wasn't until she reached this point of clarity that she was able to set herself free; a butterfly on the draft of a solitary breeze.

MOMENT OF WEAKNESS

She walked outside and stood in the rain; as if God's warm shower would dissipate the anguish, wash away the pain. She closed her eyes, searched for his face; wondering of that solitary wind; blown out of sight, so far away, to another time, another place.

The one that filled her heart, inspired her muse, penetrated completely to the core of her soul; incapable of being captured, born to be free, always on the move, lest it lose strength and die. Taking pleasure in its gusts, when she needed to reach a better place; a place of understanding, acceptance, virtue and love; where beauty was deeper than the skin, existing at the level of the soul; the bright light shown and she found warmth in its glow...

MENDING MINDS

An entire lifetime spent wandering; drifting aimlessly through the kaleidoscope that had become her life; searching always, to fill the gaping hole in her heart; mend the tear through the center of her soul; running in the shadows, through various shades of understanding; losing her self in a state of non-being, longing always for ecstatic fusion.

Given up on love and her belief that in the infinite universe there dwelled another soul that could possibly connect her own; matching her fear, torment, angst and pain; struggling with the want of peace and solace, living lost in a world of duality and change. There was no such soul; this realization leading her to see, what a lonely hunter her heart truly was; yet she continued to move forward, in an attempt to mend her own mind; the sheer weight of memory hindering at every turn.

She reached the point of hopelessness, from which she believed there was no return, falling to her knees and openly weeping; as the stars realigned, kismet interjected and he appeared before her; invisible, yet powerful in his philosophical stance; leaving her breathless in his experience and expression of life; she thanked the heavens for answering her plight and delivering this miracle.

A solitary wind that filled her completely; breathing new life into her soul; allowing trust to bloom where none had grown before; expanding to the possible; ecstasy of the sublime, revealed in the simple and ordinary; emptying herself completely, so as to be filled by his current, ready to move wherever he would take her. Her desire explicit – to evolve together into a higher, more powerful expression of themselves; drawing on the beauty, diversity, strength and weakness of each other; their connection she believed with every ounce of her being; he became her everything; the only thing that mattered.

But the wind has gone; shifted directions; on a path to therapeutic self confirmation of which she can have no part. Visions of the solitary wind haunting her mind; feeding her soul with evocation; her heart crying out in sacred prayer; an invocation of protection cast upon his spiritual journey; that the seed of conscious recognition may be awakened from the darkest depths of his wounded soul; releasing the imprisoning chains of resistance so that he may triumphantly rise and receive the delight of that which is his own light; dance with once again; not in the shadows, but in the warmth of the embracing sun.

SISTER MOON

Lightening struck and the balance was shifted; not once, but twice, and it all came down to him. He came upon her wandering barefoot in the garden, called out from beyond the shadows; and though she wasn't able to see him clearly, something rang familiar in his deliberate words and voice, causing her to pause and look in his direction.

Trusting her instincts that continually warrant believing, she invited him in and soon found him worthy; offering a key, so as to come and go as he pleased. And soon he became her own personal Jesus; happy in letting her be her self, tell her stories while filling her head; with crystalline knowledge, beliefs and perceptions that altered her course and left her second-guessing.

An unexplained peace soon settled in her soul; the storm he conjured brewed with intense passion, though the clouds were lined with sadistic cruelty; leaving her desolate and changed forever.

LOOKING ROUND

Young wanna-be Fashionista's; too cliché for a sleepy little mountain town; totally inappropriate attire, given the location and season; alabaster skin, never having been kissed by the sun.

Texting – talking – smoking; meaningless, clueless, not even inhaling; all for show, impressing no one; as she was the only one watching.

Mugs of spiced cider in lieu of a latte; would no doubt choke on her quad-shot espresso; movers and shakers with nowhere to go; on the cusp of life with no significant experience to call their own. Silly girls driven by ego; wouldn't even know what that means. Will leave the café, walkabout town, come back tomorrow and do it all again.

And there she sits, having lived twice as long; still trying to figure it out, Nietzsche beside her laptop, doing his great mind a disservice? Too many experiences, enough to share around; not wishing half of them, on even her greatest enemy.

Which has always been her self...

HUNTERS MOON

She knew the time was now, the signs all pointing to the Hunters Moon; the owl outside her window three nights in a row, crossing her path at dawn, alighting in the tree and watching as she made her way to the lake; the ring around the moon for three nights prior to the full and the broom that dropped; not once, but twice.

She was ready for the ritual; needing to do it for many reasons; the main to release her self of him; purging that which no longer served a purpose in her life, was negative in energy and influence, bringing nothing but harm and disrupting the balance she now fought so hard to maintain. The new journey had already begun; starting over, alone and unafraid, but she needed to move on; needed to breathe again. Forced to cast aside that which hindered and left her desolate, filled with pain, regret, self-loathing and doubt.

Yass…the time was now.

She gathered her tools and prepared; well aware that this would be the most intense ritual in which she would ever partake; eradicating the essence that had been selfishly burned into her very being and now possessed her soul; just as intended; complete and total, with no chance of her ever thinking about anything but him.

The red clay bowl symbolizing her flesh and blood; desert sage to drive off negative energy, spirits and influences; necessary to purify and cleanse not only her circle of stones that was carefully cast, but her self as well; the burning smoke, the breath of her prayers going out to her Creator; as she concentrated on the connection between the earth and sky and unity of all life.

Her sacrificial offering of a most personal nature; her mane of thick brown hair he once described as creating a picture that would have inspired Di Vinci; severed before the flames, in a moment of determination, sheer will and absolute power; blowing in the wind, her banner of courage, clutched in her fist and raised to the heavens, then

bundled with the stone he gave as protection, wrapped in a white shroud and buried in the earth at the center of the circle.

I will be happy forever
Nothing will hinder me
I walk with beauty before me
I walk with beauty behind me
I walk with beauty below me
I walk with beauty above me
I walk with beauty around me
My world will be beautiful

After the ritual, which left her drained of all energy, she burned a bowl of sweet grass, the most sacred of all herbs, bringing positive energy after the negative had been banished; she raised her face toward the full Hunters Moon and her voice rang out above the mountain…

Let me know peace
For as long as the moon shall rise
For as long as the rivers shall flow
For as long as the sun will shine
For as long as the grass shall grow
Let me know peace…

MY STYLE

In life and writing….

Macabre
Yearnful

Simplistic
Tenacious
Yielding
Labyrinthal
Eclectic

PRISONER OF THE FALL

A small little town, quaint in fact, once she actually ventured in and took the time to look around; but still, it felt like a temporary stop on her way to nowhere. The trees bursting in full fall regalia, before the barren grey of winter sets in, and for this natural wonder in all its simplicity, she found herself grateful.

She turned the corner and the heavenly scent of fresh roasted beans filled her senses, lightened her mood; led her to café Edmond, the only one in town. She walked in and the aroma of fresh brew mingled with wood smoke from the fireplace momentarily warmed her soul. She was greeted with smiles and friendly nods as she made her way through to the counter, where she hesitantly ordered a quad-shot latte, relieved when the gentleman responded, *"take a seat, we'll have it right up."*

She went back outside and picked a table in the sun; the waiter arrived a few minutes later with a steaming ceramic mug. She put down her bag, took a soothing drink, pulled out her laptop and began to write…

AUTUMN SAGE

They met in a little antique shop. She'd just picked up and started examining a brass stamp box when he came up behind her and said, *"Best to be careful; things aren't always what they seem."* She turned slowly, to see who the masculine voice with the slow, sultry drawl belonged to; her heart tripping in her chest as her eyes met his and held. He smiled and reached for the box, *"They sold three just like it last week,"* took it from her and set it back on the table.

"If you want to hunt for some real treasures there's a few not to be missed shoppes out along Route 9; plus the drive is a scenic knockout this time of year." As she was considering him and his bit of advice, he took her by the hand and led her outside; she followed without a word, or a moment's hesitation.

They spent three days and two nights meandering through the countryside, forests and mountain villages of Vermont, with no cares, no constraints of time and no plan; just digging the countryside and each other. He was unlike anyone she'd ever met. His ideals and philosophies sparked her thoughts and imagination like nothing or no one had done before; obviously having mingled within the upper echelon of intelligentsia, yet down to earth, genuine and real; a combination not often found.

His energy was infectious; his touch therapeutic and healing; and his uncanny knowledge of past events and talk of a certain future made her wonder if he weren't perhaps a wandering mystic Sage from one of the villages they'd passed along the way, as he was well familiar with the area and many secret places contained therein. Just as she was gathering the courage to ask, his demeanor changed, as if someone had flipped a switch and he told her it was time to return.

He was suddenly very silent, but for giving directions that led back to Route 9, until they passed the sign that read, "Welcome to Brattleboro," and that's when his dark side emerged. He began talking of death, suicide and the shithole of life, of which no one escapes unscathed. On and on he droned; nothing whatsoever like the man she believed she was coming to know.

He warned her of the sharp bend up ahead and that there would be a large wrought iron gate on the right, just past the strand of oaks. She slowed her speed and pulled into the hidden drive; an elaborately scrolled sign above the gate read, Brattleboro Retreat. She wondered if perhaps he'd changed his mind and decided to stay with her a while longer; as her mind imagined them enjoying a few languid days at what appeared to be an exclusive Vermont Inn.

Such was not the case, as they approached the small building where the guards were posted and she was escorted to a parking area off to the side by one of the guards, as he was physically removed from the car and restrained by the other. *"There's no need to question her, she knows nothing,"* she heard him say to the guard, as she demanded to know from the other just what the hell was going on.

She was quickly informed that the gentleman whose company she was in was in fact an escapee. She shot the guard a look of confusion as she shook her head, *"You mean a prisoner?"* she demanded. *"No ma'am; not a prisoner, a resident of the retreat."*

"I'm afraid I don't understand," she replied. The guard looked at her sympathetically and said, *"This is Brattleboro Retreat, ma'am; the Vermont Asylum for the Insane."*

Her heart sank in her chest and a chill crept up her spine as he called out her name and she slowly turned and met his eyes one last time. *"I warned you to be careful,"* he said with a cynical grin, *"Things aren't always what they seem….."*

COBBLESTONE AND ESPRESSO

Angular parking along cobbled streets, trucks as far as the eye can see; and a midnight blue minivan nestled in the mix, belonging to the mysterious hippie-chick; observing for weeks as she sits in lone silence; the stranger with the face slowly coming familiar.

Friendly people acknowledging, as they pass her by, all smiling and wishing her to have a nice day; wondering of her ritual that never waivers; steaming espresso, four cigarettes, seemingly disinterested as she writes in her notebook.

Trying to calm the waters that rush under her bridge, musing as the waiter delivers carafe's of hot coffee. Little birds chirp, singing for crumbs, unaware that she has none. Breaking from routine she goes back inside, ordering a piece of pumpkin bread, picking the seeds for her self.

Like Snow White in the magical forest, the birds flock, singing just for her. Thirteen gather and eat crumbs at her feet; two on the table, one brave chickadee perched proudly on her knee.

Today was quite different, breaking from routine; embracing the world she found her self in, deciding she might just stay for a spell; laughing out loud, showing traces of her true self, gathering her belongings, she left with a smile...

ALSYNA

She appeared out of nowhere at the stroke of midnight, as if having emerged from within the lake; a mirage of convenience, claiming to possess the key to get me back into the kingdom. Clearly taken aback at my hesitation, she promised to lead the entire way; guiding and navigating, until I found my self once more in the fold; where she swore I belonged, where she knew I wanted to be.

I considered her proposition momentarily, but in the end decided it just wasn't worth the wasted time and emotion, not to mention that of the pain. No, there was no going back, not now that I'd come so far; perhaps for some this was the answer, but not for me; not any more.

Too many lifetimes spent built on lies; having had my fill of traditional thinking. Not quite certain what the answer yet is, but refusing to go back to the way it was; with so-called doctors all harboring god-complexes, anxious to get their hands on you; fuck with your head, dredge up the past, reduce you to rubble and call it healing.

"Ah, but you run in circles inside your mind; thoughts that won't stop, driving you blind; and still you keep running, closer to the edge, you won't slow and yet you refuse to look back. Don't you see what you're doing, lost in this maze; it's quite clear you're holding out hope, for a miracle or a sage; perhaps a keen philosopher to enlighten as you find your way…"

I held up my hand and told her to *"Stop!"*

Enough I've had of fools and sages, and let us not forget wanna-be revolutionary thinkers; doing nothing but rehashing and pondering the thoughts of other great minds; having no faith, no ability to love, nor the courage to grasp that which is their own; far too busy obsessing the condition of life, listening to the voices that haunt their own minds; not giving a damn, or too self-absorbed to recognize, the damage caused in the wake of self-fulfilling process.

"Thank you for the offer, but I'm doing okay; certain even that one day I'll again find my way; without the influence, guidance or interference of another. Now if you don't mind, please return to the lake, leave me in peace and don't again show your face."

Shrouded in a veil of mist, Alsyna vanished just as quickly as she appeared. I turned to make my way back toward the cabin, when something on the ground shimmered and caught my attention. I walked slowly to the waters edge, bent to retrieve the item off the ground; only to find myself standing in the moonlight, with an all-too-real key resting in my hand…

COUNTER CLOCKWISE

She watched the pendulum swaying; back-and-forth, back-and-forth, the incessant ticking once maddening now soothing, almost comforting; a constant beacon to cling to when the light faded and her world turned to black; but the beacon an illusion, just as time itself. A man-made tracking device used to run our lives by; but insignificant in the scheme of existence, as we edge ever so closer to the precipice of reality.

And in her mind she heard the chime, ringing out upon the hour, the half-hour and that delicate tune whenever the doorbell was pressed; the main focal point upon entering the foyer; bejeweled adornments gracing their wrists, worn on chains or pinned to lapels. All consuming, ruling their lives; moving too quickly, conscious of its ever-present looming, watching helplessly as it passed them by.

In the end with nothing left to cling to, no hope of ever leaving alive; they did the only thing then knew, trying to buy themselves more time. A simple truth not to be grasped in the whole long lot of their lives; that time could not be bought in any form.

Yet the magnificently expensive grandfather clock chimes upon the hour, bearing witness to life's long arduous journey; gracing the lobby of the old folk's home, with their names etched upon a plate of gold.

THE POWER OF WORDS

Her mind overflowed with thoughts of him, as she woke to face another day; fragments from dreams, carried into consciousness; longing so intense it made her weep. Moments of certainty, clarity and light, clutched at her heart like a constricting vice; then shadowed suddenly, as cruel words came back to haunt her; the end relived, mocked by his meanness.

Feeling numb, longing for darkness, she stumbled upon words that shifted her perception...

"One's dignity may be assaulted, vandalized and cruelly mocked, but it cannot be taken away unless it is surrendered" ~Morton Kondrake

SIXGUINESS

He offered up a quote, a less cynical Goethe; about noble men, helpful and good; set apart from every other creature on earth; and while she appreciated the gesture, she found no comfort in the words; for cynical is the heart, having been given and held, then without warning viscously broken and bled; at the hand of a madman with no conscience to speak of.

WITCHING HOUR

She sat in darkness before a blank screen; mind numb from endless thoughts turning, as her entire world had become since his departure. Her abysmal writing proof that mediocrity is alive and well in a world that has forgotten what great literature is about; his words slashing like swords, haunting her day and night, blocking the flow she had come to count on.

Taken them too, her words, her solace; left her in the dark, stumbling with nothing. Her only reprieve found in the witching hour, knowing that after midnight they would forever be the same; left in loneliness to suffer fates pain.

MISSING THEM

Her hand in mine
So soft and small
His bear hungs
Belly laughs
Thinning hair

Only traces remain
Her scent on
The quilt
Pottery bowl
Filled with his
Change

Happy they came
Sad to watch
Them go
Can't wait
To see them
Again

Feels like
Forever
Until Spring
Will come
Counting the
Days
Looking forward
To home

LUNATIC FRINGE

It is no accident that she sees these things, these glimpses of the future and what lies behind the veil of façade in which some choose to linger. There are no accidents and they always seem to come at an appropriate time in her life; just when she needs the clarity most, but still, always surprising and completely unexpected.

She knew there was a certain level of craziness in him, but wanted to believe it was more of a rebelliousness than actual lunacy; although he claimed to be insane more than once, almost to the point of bragging; as if being insane and unable to control his thoughts and function in society was something to be proud of; an achievement of those with superior intelligence and knowledge. He was intelligent, of that there was no doubt; and strange enough, it was his mind and perception of life that attracted her in the first place, which left her wondering of her own mental stability in the end.

He preached change, was obsessed with changing, always claiming to have or be in process of changing; but people like him don't change, just talk a good line of bullshit and continue wandering aimlessly; alone, taking up space and doing absolutely nothing for the greater good of mankind, and leaving a trail of destruction and debris in their wake.

She saw him walking the streets along the bay; baggy shorts, sandals and a Hawaiian touristy shirt; a 180 pound chic magnet in tow, in the form of a St. Bernard named Bud. He looked just as he had, but older with rougher edges and quite a bit heavier and wider; still talking his crap, looking for the next big score; still no pot to piss in or window to throw it out of; no longer able to count on his looks and words to lure them on his own, letting Bud do the work of hooking them, as he tried his damndest to reel them in.

Eventually they all stopped listening and even in darkness he couldn't find peace, as the voices in his head refused to stop taunting. He lived a life of loneliness, claiming to have wanted it that way, but he was a liar and a con, left to reap exactly what he had sown. Unable to hold even the most menial of jobs; no money to feed himself or his dog, he wandered the streets panhandling, with that single copy of the book he had penned, designed and produced years ago by a chic whose name he'd long since forgotten; pages yellowed and dog-eared, no one listening to the raving lunatic, who stood on the corner and read excerpts aloud, from the book by an author no one ever heard of.

SIDE AFFECTS

I didn't know what to say; everyone was shocked when they heard, devastated really, at the tragedy of it all; everyone but me that is.

I said nothing when they told me, remained completely numb and emotionless; not because I wasn't saddened by the loss, but because I saw it coming; warned her even, but she didn't listen; was way past the point of caring what others said or thought; totally out of control, careening down the road of destruction; in this case death.

It was as if the moment he left, she slipped into a state of denial and depression. Not to say she wasn't ready to start a new chapter in her life, but I think it was the way he left that affected her so. They'd been together way too long, taking each other for granted, slipping into routine and accepting the comfortableness of their life along with the dysfunction; because it was easier to just let it go than to actually let go and move on. But he had had enough; told her he wanted out and that's what crushed her ego and drove her to this madness.

She sought medical attention after a few months of non-living and was given medication, warned of its side affects and dangers and cautioned not to mix with alcohol or any other drugs; soon thereafter her alter-ego emerged; as if someone had flipped a switch inside her mind and then wound the gears too tight.

I didn't believe it at first, when she told me she'd met a carnie working the state fair. I laughed and only when I saw the hurt in her eyes did I know that she was serious. Now don't get me wrong, I've never been one to believe that we're defined by what we do for a living, but when she showed me the picture of him she'd snapped with her phone, I knew my misgivings were not off the mark.

She only saw him twice, but that turned out to be one time too many. They found her body in the woods less than a mile from the fairgrounds; raped, mutilated and decomposing; a stuffed pink pig on the ground beside her, an obvious prize from one of the midway games, with traces of cotton candy and blood under her fingernails. Her four kids who were once her entire world, will now be raised by their grandparents; and forever left to wonder what really happened to their mother, as the woman killed was not the embodiment of the mother they knew and loved.

INTERVENTION

Some say she's
Losing it
Spiraling out of
Control

Others say
This is the
"Real her"
Just coming
To light

Regardless
Which version
Is real
It's embarrassing
To watch

Not only
Is she not
All that
She's not that
At all

But no one
Stops her
They just
Smile
Pretending
It's not
Happening

Who
Am I
To tell her
Any different

AUTUMNAL FAUST

She thought he was an angel, swirling round her spirit; arousing a creative fire; igniting bursts of imagination and stoking profound inner realizations. She breathed deep, a sigh of relief, at having connected with one so astute in realms that piqued her interests; then as if daring her to be great, he forced her to open her self to experience a new perception; and glimpsing the possibilities, she didn't hold back.

A spontaneous passion for truth emerged; transforming her imaginative insights and work into a receptacle of spiritual artistry. She believed…quite possibly for the first time, that there was no limit to what she could achieve; striving to understand and contact the highest part of her being, in which the impetus for pure expression of art and life resides.

But he came not, bathed in the light of life with a mirrored goal in mind, but rather in self-annihilation with the purpose, intent and pragmatic outlook at what he believed needed to be obtained; could be obtained…at whatever cost.

The vision of truth, beauty and ecstasy a falsity she would be forced to cast out of her memory; as this was anything but a soulful new beginning, as led to believe; but the start of one very long arduous journey; but as with all things in life, there are no accidents and chance meetings; and so it was left to her to sift through the rubble, for traces of lessons she could take away with her, while the remaining debris was left to scatter to the wind; the winds of change.

QUOTE OF THE DAY

"She saw madness in his eyes; and still she did not fear him…"

[from- Autumnal Faust]

MEMORIES PAST

It was about this time of year; I remember the barren trees and the rain; the cold November rain…

We were on our way home, it was pouring, and as we rounded the sharp curve at the bottom of the hill we could see the skid marks and the mangled guardrail where someone had gone off the side of the bridge into the creek. We pulled over and as my dad jumped out of the car, I wiped the window with my sleeve to try to clear the fog; and through the rain stained glass I could see the underside of a truck with its wheels sticking up out of the rushing water, where it had flipped and landed on its top. I stepped out into the pouring rain when my dad jumped the guardrail and disappeared over the side of the bridge; and that's when I heard her voice.

I couldn't see where she was, but she screamed for me to get help. I stood, paralyzed in fear, watching my dad try to rescue the driver who was trapped in the truck; and then I realized the voice was that of my classmate, Missy, and the person trapped in the truck was her mother.

I took off up the road, running to the farmhouse at the top of the hill where another one of our schoolmates lived; her voice filled with desperation, calling out from behind me, *"Run Jill, run…"* over and over…and I did; I ran like the wind; fear and adrenaline pushing me on, up the hill through the driving rain. When I reached the house I was a trembling, soaking, frightened mess. They told me they'd already called 911 and then continued talking amongst themselves. I stood there, my eleven year old mind in shock; never having been subjected to something so tragic, devastating and surreal. I remember saying,

"That's my dad down there…that's her mom; that creek always floods; he's got to get her out!" and they ignored me as if I weren't even there.

In a daze, I slowly made my way back down the hill along the shoulder of the road. The cold rain mixed with my hot tears stinging my eyes. I was halfway down when I heard the sirens, a moment later the flashing lights. I stopped where I was; not wanting to get too close; not wanting to see what was happening, feeling the hand of death reaching out, praying to a God I barely knew that it wasn't so.

I don't remember the exact moment my dad reappeared, I don't remember seeing Missy at all; I don't remember if we stayed there with her or left and went home. I just remember hearing someone say that her mothers head was caught between the back of the seat and the window and it was too late, that her windpipe was crushed; and she was dead.

It was awkward when she finally returned to school. I didn't know what to say, I felt as if I'd somehow let her down; and I remember it was hard for me to look her in the eye. They moved not too long after, and I clearly remember the guilt I felt at not having told her how I felt before she left; how sorry I was that her mother had died; sorry for not running faster and for my dad not being able to save her. I suppose in my young subconscious mind I believed that nothing I could say would make the slightest difference, and at that age maybe it wouldn't have.

But I still hold the memory of that fateful day that altered two young lives and minds forever; different in scope and depth, but both altered nonetheless; and as long as I live I'll never forget the sound of her voice calling out to me through the rain…

GRATEFUL

I never understood how it was that he could wake up in such a foul mood. Before his feet even hit the floor he was growling at the world; as if being given another day was somehow a curse he was forced to endure. He loathed life; I truly believe that now, and no matter what I said or did to try to make his world a better place, it only seemed to make it worse.

I think over time he came to loathe me as well; for wanting to see the good in people, being satisfied with the simple things in life, seeing beauty in the world around me, for refusing to wallowing with him in hate and despair; and for eventually realizing enough was enough and moving on with my life.

I'm so grateful that chapter of my life is over...

THE PAWN BREAKER

Blinded
　By pain
　　I could
Suddenly see

His lunacy
　His lies
　　His penchant
For debauchery

Life is his
　Game
　　People merely
His pawns

To get what
　He needs
　　Incapable
On his own

KARMIC DESTINY

A few weeks ago he was a homeless vagabond; sleeping on couches of friends kind enough to invite him in, and in the beds of those unwitting enough to have him. In all honesty he has no true friends; only the ones crazy enough to put up with his insanity and those he can get something out of; be it a place to crash, a pinch of their stash or borrowed cash, does he call friends; though he'd fuck them over in a moments notice if need be and move on without a second thought; and those whose bed he shares; nothing more than faceless masturbation when he's too lazy to do it himself. Thus was the way of this self-proclaimed sociopath with no sense of moral responsibility or conscience to speak of.

He'd d been searching for work, running on empty and needed to turn the tables quick. So he placed a free ad on an online dating service; posted fluff and stuff about his lonely heart, a decade old photo and poetic prose about the love songs he longed to create for the right woman if she came along. Within hours they were taking the bait.

He hit pay-dirt with a bipolar cutie just a few miles outside of town, met her for coffee, feigned love at first site, and by the end of the week he was schlepping his bags to her house. She mentioned she had a kid, but that wasn't going to deter him; he needed a place to settle for a spell while he tried to find himself once again; tired of being a nameless phantom wandering cold lonely streets leading to nowhere; needing to find the right path, get his name and work out there.

The house was a small two-bedroom, neatly kept, but crowded nonetheless. The kid stayed out of his way, didn't say much, but kept his eyes and ears peeled; he knew the drill, as this wasn't the first stray his mother had brought home, but he was prepared to make this psycho the last; for this one got comfortable just a little to quick, was by far the most arrogant and condescending son of a bitch and wore a look of lunacy worse than any of the rest.

They gathered in the yard one day after school, the kid and two of his closest friends; no longer boys, not yet men, having led bullshit lives, indignant to the world around them, not caring from right or wrong; left to fend for themselves by no-good, worthless parents. Having had enough, they prepared to take a stand.

They made their way inside, knowing the lunatic boyfriend would still be asleep having just landed a dead-end gig working third shift. They watched as he stirred when the door creaked slowly open, pushed at his pillow and rolled over without waking. They rifled his knapsack, pawned his laptop and gave the janitor ten bucks and two buds to burn what was left in the school incinerator.

He never saw it coming, hadn't a clue what was happening, and with one quick blow to the head, his lights went out forever; the nameless phantom, cascading the shaft of a backyard well; fading unknown into eternal mist.

MISS MAE-MAE

She was in the courtyard shucking oysters for the stuffing, when the old woman came shuffling out the kitchen door; her empty basket hooked over her arm, heading straight for the garden to dig turnips and pick fresh greens. It was the first time she'd accepted Trey and Nan's invitation to join them for Thanksgiving; and while the thought of spending the holiday alone, in that cozy mountain cabin by the fire was something she'd actually been looking forward to; from the moment she woke in that beautiful Victorian guestroom, the sound of a horse drawn carriage on the cobblestone streets outside her window, she was glad she'd come.

She was up before the rest of the house and made her way across four squares to River Street to walk along the water; the city blanketed in eerie silence; the only stirrings were of ghostly apparitions having wandered the night, returning to the cold tombs of her imagination.

Ah, Savannah…the place her soul knows as home.

The old woman filled her basket then made her way over to observe the shucking. She sat down on the bench with her basket in her lap; "We certainly are blessed to be here on this fine day, wouldn't you say?" The young woman looked up and smiled, "Any day in Savannah is a beautiful day, no?" The old woman chuckled, "I suppose you're right. I don't believe we've had the pleasure…I'm Trey's grandma, folks call me Mae-Mae," she said as she removed her gardening glove and held out a delicately small, wrinkled hand. "Very nice to meet you, Miss Mae-Mae; I'm Shelby."

They shook hands and Shelby continued shucking, as the woman intently watched. "Don't get me wrong honey, I'm grateful Trey and Nan invited you and we have the opportunity to share this day, but I can't help but wonder why you're not with your own family." Shelby looked up, met the old woman's eyes that despite their age, still sparkled like gems and forced a smile, wondering exactly what Nan and Trey had told her.

She was contemplating an answer when Mae-Mae looked off over the courtyard, raised her face to the sun and said, "Seems to me, married folk these days give up way too easy. I was married for sixty-seven years before my Rupert passed on. Oh, we had a time of it, ups-and-downs like a rollercoaster it seemed at times, but at the end of the day, when the sun went down, no matter what we'd endured, we knew we could make it through, because we had each other."

She sat silent for a moment then continued, "Oh, sure, I hear them talk; how different it is these days, how the world isn't the same place it used to be, but honey, I can tell you in all certainty, that while times may have changed, people haven't."Shelby said nothing; her mind a mass of swirling images, of all the rights and wrongs having happened over the past six months that had led her to where she was now.

Mae-Mae stood slowly and offered one final bit of wisdom. "All of us wonder, at one time or another, just how green the grass really is on the other side. Some stand at the fence and wonder their whole lives, never satisfied, simply because they never knew; while others of us *need* to jump the fence; for in doing so, it's the only way to move forward, the only way we can truly begin to grow.

"What lies on the other side, no one can be sure of, not until they've actually been; and the sad truth is, most are disappointed once they get there, destroying what they once had, never getting the chance to go back; but for a few truly blessed and truly loved, who find barren fields and a sunless sky, the gate remains open, never having been closed."

Shelby wiped the tears from her eyes and watched as Mae-Mae slowly made her way back inside, touched by the wisdom of the aged. It wasn't the first time she'd come across an elder offering such clear direction, and she was certain it wouldn't be the last. She knew in her heart it was time to go home; run through the gate and mend her fences.

Later that evening, as they gathered for their Thanksgiving feast, Shelby noticed that not only were there no turnips or greens, but that Mae-Mae was missing as well. When she questioned Trey, assuming she was resting in her room and asked if she might take her a plate, his face grew pale and tears filled his eyes. Shelby was taken aback by his reaction, wondering suddenly if she'd said something wrong.

Nan reached over to comfort her husband, looked at Shelby and said simply, "Mae-Mae is no longer with us; she passed away Thanksgiving day…..four years ago."

B F F

I missed her birthday; first time in thirty-seven years. I wonder if she can forgive me. I wonder if she would understand if I were to tell her that while I thought of her, I simply hadn't the will to get out of bed, go out into the world, into the store and read through a plethora of cards, when I had no sentiment in me; blinded by my own darkness, searching for the light; lost in an abyss of loneliness and angst, trying to wrap my head around truth, for all the lies.

An endless stream of bittersweet lies…

I can see clearly now, for the fog has lifted; and while I still feel bad for not reaching out on her day, I cannot help but wonder why we do it. Nine years since we've seen each other and probably twenty since I knew what was in her head, in her heart.

Inseparable once upon a time, drifted apart on the current of life, landing on opposite shores. I wonder what trials and tribulations she's faced in hers, if they in any way match my own. Somehow I doubt it, though I'm probably wrong. We were similar creatures growing up; living on opposite sides of the tracks, but on the same street nonetheless. But we lost something along the way and though we've talked over the years, it seems meaningless, forced and incredibly contrived; stuck in the past, when we are no longer those girls, but women who have yet to be properly introduced.

MISSING THE POINT

If she leaves a message, I purposely email her back, just so I don't have to talk to her. She's the type that knows something about everything and is more than happy to share her font of knowledge, whether you want to hear it or not; droning on and on, mercilessly, until your ears begin to bleed; even then she doesn't stop talking; she'll offer a tissue to dab the blood, but her mouth is moving a million miles a minute as she's doing it.

So, imagine my horror when I walked in the ladies room and found her at the sink. I couldn't very well ignore her, pretending as though I hadn't seen her; although for a split-second I thought about grabbing my stomach, doubling over and running for the nearest stall as if my life depended on it, but I just knew she'd stand there and talk to me through the stall walls. So I said hello and instead of leaving it at that asked how she was, to which she burst out in tears and a never-ending stream of explanation spewed forth…

Her husband's job was just cut to 20 hours; she'd always been the bread-winner but they were now starving; working endless hours to get the deals on the table for her clients, only to have them fall through for one reason or another. She held up her blackberry, looked at it, told me how much she pays for it each month and wondered if she could get by without it; but then she wouldn't have the convenience of holding her world in the palm of her hand; she'd actually have to be at a desk to take her calls; sitting in front of a computer to check and answer emails; nope, can't do without the $200 a month blackberry!

Perhaps they could get rid of one of their cars, but that means she'd have to drive him to work, be there to pick him up; and Christmas! What were they going to do about Christmas?! That's when the faucet of tears was turned on high; the thought of having to call her family, admit that they were struggling and couldn't afford Christmas gifts for everyone! That's when I held up my hand and interrupted; "Christmas isn't about giving gifts, don't you realize that?" she looked at me as if I'd lost my mind.

I asked if she thought about taking a family picture and putting it in a Christmas card, penning a personal note and calling it a gift. "Oh, we can't afford to have a family portrait taken right now." Missing my point entirely and scrunching her nose when I explained that I was talking about a candid snapshot of the family.

I then spewed forth my own thoughts, which left her momentarily speechless; hoping to give her something to go away thinking about.

The fact that she wasn't alone in her strife; that the whole nation is facing economic hard times and that if this doesn't prove, yet again, who's really in charge, then what will?! What better place to hit than where it hurts; and sadly that being our bank accounts, the only way to truly get our attention. Proving once again that we're a spoiled, selfish and lazy people, driven by greed, convenience and material possessions; forcing us to reassess our lives, shift our priorities, make due with what we have, counting our blessings as we do, and getting back to the heart of what is truly important in this life.

She looked at me and said, "Who's in charge?"

I turned and walked out of ladies room without saying another word...

HER NAME WAS DOWANHOWEE

"The utmost good faith shall always be observed toward the Indians, their lands and property shall never be taken from them without their consent; and in their property, rights and liberty, they shall never be invaded or disturbed, unless in just and lawful wars authorized by Congress; but laws founded in justice and humanity shall from time to time be made, for preventing wrongs being done to them, and for preserving peace and friendship with them."

-Article III of the Northwest Ordinance

I never knew, in my life, a time when the white man was not at odds with my people, yet I was raised on memories of when my people lived free; free as the Buffalo that roamed the land; free to hunt and gather the bounties that Mother Earth provided. We did not take more than was needed and gave thanks for what was received. We lived in peace among each other and cherished the sacred lands of our elders; land that the white man would eventually take from us.

In the beginning there were only a few; settlers that we watched from high atop the hills; their covered wagons making their way across the valley; but soon more came, and instead of moving on, they remained among us, because of the gold rock that grew in the Black Hills.

They spoke of treaties we did not fully understand, and fearful for the survival of our people, the elders agreed to them; but soon it wasn't enough. In all their greed an animosity, the treaties they made, they eventually broke; taking the land for themselves and dividing our people. We were confined to several small reservations, forced to farm, raise livestock and send our children to boarding schools, where they were stripped of their culture and Native language, in an attempt, they explained, to cleanse the souls of the heathens.

They did not for one minute, take into account our way of life, our beliefs and ways of prayer, believing instead that theirs was the only way; determined that if we must co-exist, they would take whatever steps necessary to improve us, by removing what they saw as faults and unacceptable behaviors; improving us by forcing their methods and values upon us.

The growing season was a time of little rain and much sun; the land incapable of producing the crops they would have us grow and cultivate, but the white man refused to listen to reason, called us lazy Indians, rather than admit that their plan had failed. Soon they cut our rations in half and our people began to starve. We did the only thing we could do; we prayed to our spirit elders in the form of the Ghost Dance; seeking answers and guidance in our time of desperate need. The white man feared what they did not understand and believed our ceremony was the signal of an uprising and soon thousands more came to the reservations.

We fled Standing Rock when word of the killing of Sitting Bull reached us; seeking refuge with the last great chief, Red Cloud, in one of the few remaining Ghost Dance camps. The Sioux leaders met with Red Cloud and it was agreed that the only means of survival was to surrender to the white man; and so we prepared for the journey to Pine Ridge Agency in South Dakota, but before the journey began, were met with 500 troops of the U.S. 7th Cavalry, who surrounded our encampment with orders to use force if necessary, to escort us to the railroad for transport to Nebraska

Before proceeding they had orders to disarm the tribesmen; during the process, Black Coyote, a tribesman who was deaf and did not understand the orders being given, refused to give up his rifle. The white man took this as a sign of defiance; that coupled with the fear and misunderstanding of the Ghost Dance they had witnessed when they came upon our encampment, were certain we were preparing for battle.

Those simple misunderstandings set off a chain of reactions, as a single gunshot rang out and fighting began between both sides; but most of the Sioux had been unarmed, and so fled for their lives, in a scene of chaos, mayhem and terror, as the troops shot at anyone and everyone, many a point-blank range.

By the time it was over, more than 300 men, women and children of the Lakota Sioux lay dead. It was believed that 150 succeeded in fleeing unharmed, only to die an agonizing death in the freezing cold of the wilderness into which they had escaped. Several of us they deemed survivors, lay wounded in the back of the Calvary wagon in the freezing cold and snow. It would be hours before they came to take us away. I remember fading in and out of darkness, finding peace from my physical and mental wounds in the blackness, my mind unable to release the images of my people; helpless, defenseless, falling dead all around me.

I saw a far away light that I focused on, for what seemed like forever, as we traversed the land and I was taken farther and farther away; leaving my broken heart with my dead people, at the place that would come to be known as the sacred battleground of Wounded Knee.

And then I was being lifted from the wagon, into the arms of the enemy. I realized we had been taken to a church, the holy place of the white man; and I remember well the warmth from within wrapping itself around me like a blanket. I was taken inside and placed on the floor, the forlorn faces of their women forever etched in my memory as they looked upon me, not knowing what to do; fearful of me, as they had come to be taught, but sympathetic nonetheless. And I looked up and saw the banner hanging at the front of the room, bearing the message from their Lord and Savior; wondering how such a simple, straightforward message, could be so easily forgotten. ...

"Peace on Earth, Good Will toward Men..."

SUNDAY SURPRISE

Phone rings
Sweet
Hello

Breakfast bar
Bellies
Full

Grandma's car
Speaker
Phone

Check balance
Papa's
Giftcards

Giggling girls
Sitting
Waiting

Aunt Jilly
So
Silly

Mimicking voices
Burping
Crapola

Searching site
Highspeed
Internet

Laughing still
Singing
Jingle-bells

Balances checked
Twenty-five
Ten

Unknown lingo
Venti
Bold

Bye Aunt-Jilly
Gotta
Go

Drop-off babies
Starbucks
Ho

L'ESPRIT DE PARIS

Feeling old, past her prime, out of the loop as it were; sitting in solitude, quiet contemplation; sipping pink spirits, sweet nectar de Paris; watching from a distance, always at a distance; some foolhardy, others a disgrace, but no two the same and none of particular interest.

When in the wee hours he came, from his Technicolor world; into the vast unknown, unwittingly into hers. To an island nestled deep, in the Aegean Sea; where all men are naked and women mate with the gods. A miraculous place, where the curvature of the universe was visible from the shore; galaxies unfurled onto one another, time was irrelevant and spirits flew tangible, so as to no longer be illusive.

Though danger lurked deep, in light as well as shadows and as was her nature, she dove headlong without thinking; into a world she didn't belong, where death was eminent and the coming slow and painful.

She stumbled blind, round that last corner; seeking death or redemption, at that moment it made no difference. A familiar face, his beauty betraying his sin, on 185 horses he roared in like the wind. The dark knight of her days come to save her from harm; those who chased and that of her own; sages and soothsayers and a convoluted self-image.

Shocked to find him there, though she hesitated nary a moment, as he led her by the hand to a safe and secluded place; revealing all that she refused to think and never dared to dream. Heart pounding in sweet trepidation, as he slowly rose above, filling her completely, body and soul; coming inside with an explosion of color, matching then surpassing that which emanated his skin.

IN THIS SILENCE

Too many used to be's
Faded away with
Time

Not enough now's
To sustain us
Into tomorrow

IN DREAMS

I came upon him in the woods; sitting on a bench nestled among a patch of wild ferns growing along the trail; dapples of sunlight playing on his face. I could tell, even behind sunglasses that his eyes were closed in quiet contemplation. Perhaps it was the tilt of his head or the relaxed posture of his shoulders; regardless, though I was surprised and delighted to find him there, I didn't want to intrude.

I stood for a moment in silence, watching him; still trying to grasp the fact that he was actually there, when he patted the empty spot on the bench next to him and said, "Why don't you come sit." Only then, when I took a step toward him, did he look in my direction and smile.

"What are you doing here," I asked. "What took you so long," he replied.

I sat beside him; and after a moments hesitation I humbly answered, "I thought he was a sage, sent to help me find my way; turns out he was insane, and I, nothing but a pawn in one of his wicked games." He shook his head slowly, as if he understood completely. "What exactly was it you were hoping to find?" I shrugged my shoulders, but he wasn't buying it; still, I didn't know what to say.

We sat for several minutes, basking in the natural wonders surrounding us; each lost in separate thought, both thinking the same thing.

"It's easy to see that you're on the right path; you just need to have a little more faith is all; but I can tell that faith doesn't come easy for you, does it?" I shook my head, but said nothing. He took my hand

and held it in his, "While I can't guide you in matters of faith, I'll be happy to help you in mastering your craft."

"And how will you do that," I finally asked. "By encouraging when you stumble, flounder and flail, and watching as you flourish, spread your wings and sail. I've been here all along, I'm not going anywhere; and if you allow me, I'll be your confidant and friend..."

I moved a little closer, leaned my head on his shoulder; took a deep breath and let out a slow sigh of relief. "Thank you, Walter," I whispered in my sleep.

TRANQUILITY

Sitting in the dark
Listening to silence
Lights from the Christmas tree
Illuminating the room

RESOLUTION

No regrets
No looking back
Both feet on the path
Forging ahead -

AND SO IT GOES...

She undressed her mind and succumbed to the illusion of what might have lifetimes ago been; the fantasy of what the future could be, dancing in delight to the fanciful notion that momentarily was.

Ample time has passed; necessary to digest, dissect, research and analyze. Emotion in check, clear vision and intent; time to put pen to paper and do what she does best.

And so she sits back, in that quiet cafe; lights dim, music soothing, fire crackling, espresso steaming; vintage fountain pen in hand, leather-bound hand tooled journal in her lap; where she will tell her tale, weave the spell, cast a light into the face of madness once again.

Musing at the lengths she sometimes goes; to snag a soul in wandering flight, reel in gently so as to cause no harm, and extract the story that lingers within; waiting to be set free, for the world to see; page after page, just as it should be.

CONVERSATION AND A QUOTE

I couldn't help but laugh, as I was telling him what I heard; I'm not used to being around them in such close proximity, and I swear she sounded just like Snoop Dog's wife, Shante; nearly stopped me dead in my tracks, but I knew better and kept on walking; closing the door to my office behind me, turning up the jazz and pretending I didn't hear what I'd just heard.

"There's a reason you're in to all your Zen stuff...if you weren't, the whole world would be off balance." Then if I'm not mistaken, I believe he called me a goof-ball. Wonder what he meant by that....

HOLLOW SOUL

Like a tree
Solid strong
Broad and stocky
Hollow at the
Core
Rotten inside

Peering leering
Paranoid searching
Driven by
Ego
Googling his own
Name

Empty of
Feeling
Driven by
Madness
Writing his
Life
In poetry and
Prose

Found on pages
Endless pages
Dostoevsky
Bukowski
Kerouac
Neitzsche

Incapable of
Grasping
All forms of
Reality
Stories already
Told

A life of
Emulation
Lost in theirs
Unconscious of
Time
Forever living
The lie

VAST AND POTENT

He went by
Many names
Though I never
Called him
Any

His reach was
Vast and potent
Though it lasted
For no time
At all

It amazed and
Dazzled
Then fizzled and
faded

Not unlike that
Of a fireworks
Display

And though my
Heart
Has long since
Forgotten
My muse still
Holds on
Strong

MAD GAB

Enjoying my espresso, southern breeze warm on my face; Sinatra
crooning holiday tunes softly in the background, laptop on the table
and Tula Belle at my side, patiently waiting for a mini vanilla scone.

My sanctuary invaded; three women meeting for coffee; frivolous
banter of Christmas shopping sprees, 75% off sales, work-related
bitching and high-pitched squeals of laughter. Holiday themed
sweaters and jackets, the kind my grandma used to wear; no older than
me, yet already set in their old lady ways; shut the fuck up, I want to
scream!

I light a smoke, my espresso now tepid, the smoke wafts their way and
they look at me in scorn. Perhaps it will be enough to make them go
away, and I can get back to the business of writing, in my corner of
sanctity, just me and my girl…

REDEMPTIVE CONTENTMENT

She fled his
Love
Not once but twice
Following a
Heart
Laden with lies

He never asked
For her madness
Yet withstood
The wrath diligently

She will gladly
Spend
The rest of her days
Loving him
Completely

She owes him
Nothing less
While he deserves
So much
More

WINTER MORN

Can't breathe
Ice crystals burning
Hitting the warmth of inflated lungs

ABSOLUTION

They're obviously concerned; having brought it up twice. Something they wish they had done when she was a small child; something they claim she needs to do now.

Why the urgency, she wonders to herself; do they sense her death, lingering close at hand? Has she fallen so far off their paved and perfect path, that they feel the sudden need to absolve themselves?

And if she were to baptize her self, in those just and sacred waters; would God be watching? Would He even care?

SINS OF MAN

They were a strange lot; the great-grands in the center with their brood all around; filling three pews on the far left of the church. Two daughters, each producing a set of twins; one had boys, the other girls; of each set, one was perfectly normal, the other not so much. Strange genetics; that each daughter should not only produce a set of twins, but that one of those twins was mentally defective; and the air of superiority that hung above them like a cloud; something I never quite understood, but gave little thought to.

As I grew older, however, I deduced that it was the ones that hid the most skeletons in their closet that carried this air; and since neither daughter's husband ever showed face at church or any of the social functions, I assumed this was the cause. For women who were faithful church-goers, unable to conform their husbands, often had an attitude about them that was unbecoming and not easily ignored; as if they felt it necessary to prove themselves holy worthy and above the rest. Never made sense to me, but then little about that church ever did.

Like the people who showed up twice a year; at Easter and Christmas, decked to the nines, surpassing the rest to take their place in the front row; the offering plate dipping low, as they placed that big fat check in; believing the entrance to heaven was something to be bought and not earned; or the old ladies that smiled to your face then cursed you the minute they passed through the doors; the stoop outside, apparently fair ground, where anything goes; unseen and unheard.

And so imagine the revelation, when upon his death-bed, the young daughter of a distant relative of the clan, (I'm still uncertain of the actual family connection), not only refused to go to hospital and pay her last respects to "Grandpa Darby," who had not only been an upstanding member of the church, but a devoted family man as well, but broke down, telling a horrific tale of things he had done to her when she was but a wee helpless girl.

As I understand it, shortly after his death, the Matriarch of the family packed up her daughters and incestual clan; fleeing the church and town they called home, never to be seen or heard from again; while the courageous girl who came forth with the truth is still in therapy, suffering bouts of depression and three unsuccessful suicide attempts.

All those lives, touched and tainted, by one wicked old man who now rots in the ground. Nothing was ever said of it in church, though there were hushed whispers all around; a perfect opportunity for a sermon with meaning as far as I was concerned; but the pastor had no balls and instead of confronting the truth, chose to sweep it under the rug.

It was then that my faith finally wavered, my beliefs in organized religion changed forever...

THE HYENA

It wasn't his
Voice
Finally found
After fifty years
Of living
Dead

It was his
Imitation skills
Finely tuned
Honed
Down pat

Poetry, prose
Letters and
Madness
No original
Thought
Merely mimicking
Bukowski's style

The scruples
Morals
By which he
Lives his
Life
Memorized passages
Dog-eared
Pages

Following
A script
Assuming a
Personal role
Worse than
Any
Fictional whore

Tinkering with
Lives
Pissing on
Souls
Watching emotionless
Counting the
Score

Take it off
The shelf
Read it once
More
Soulless bastard
Thinks he's
Hank Chinaski

GRIPPING NUMBESS

I remember those winters well; when the world turns a negative shade of grey, the suns vibrance diminishes to a bright, blinding white and the cold wraps around and holds you hostage. Seemingly surrounded by death at best; as depression settles deep within the confines of my soul; futile attempts, searching for a way out; hindered by storms of snow and ice; madness wrapping around, crippling my mind; inaudible screams driving me blind.

A distant, frigid memory; as I bask in the embrace of the warm southern sun; my soul awash in each colorful sunrise; hope-filled rays reflecting ocean waves; coloring my world, stimulating imagination; restoring my muse, from the brink back to life.

I revel in this sanctity; ever aware of those distant dreams and frost-bitten memories; the gripping numbness beneath the moon of madness; and that looming presence that brought me to this sanity...

ENDLESS NOTHING

Sea fog rolling
So thick
You can watch it
Coming

When it hits
Leaves you
Standing

Surrounded
By a void
Of endless
Nothing

A K I N

...and so I was reminded, that each of them had suffered; in various ways and to differing degrees of agony and pain. Infected with a unique version of the strand, but the same virus nonetheless...

HYPOCRITIC BULLSHIT

So tired of people…

Screaming for love
When there's no love
In them

Crying foul
When they cheat
At every turn

Pointing a finger
Casting the
Blame

Refusing to take
Responsibility
For actions all
Their own

Refusing or
Unable

A sure sign
Of the true
Make-up

Is it any
Wonder
I chose this
Path of
Darkness

Blinded by the
Light
When true colors
Are revealed

GONE MISSING

My muse has fled
In search of lost
Words
Untold stories
Unexplored worlds

In anxious
Desperation
I patiently
Wait
Return she will
In her own
Sweet time

Bringing gifts
Stimulating my
Mind
Enough to fill
This void
Inside

BACKWOODS BUCKS

Six hundred twenty nine miles
A little town called Caryville
Where goats are chained
In the yard with the dogs

The circle of sustenance
Shot up from the treetops
Nestled in the foothills
Shiny brand new

Out the door
Quint venti white mocha
Bottle of syrup $6.99
Never have I traveled
So far for a fix

CAPTURED MOMENT

Cluster of blue
Drifting
A rainy grey
Backdrop

Traffic at a
Standstill
Three lanes
Wide

Following its
Motion
While forced
To sit
Idle

Watching
Wondering
The cause of
Celebration

Birthday
Anniversary
Farewell
Hello

Are they floating
Deliberate
Let loose to
The sky

Happy to
Watch
In mind-numbing
Madness

As they drift
Past my
Window
No matter

WASTED AWAY

Years spent. Surrounded by his hatred. Wasted. Euphoric highs one minute, terrifying lows the next. Wondering too often if I'd make it out alive; or simply drown in the shallows of his dysfunction; his sickness; his disease. Refusing treatment, medicating with reefer; to make the world a better place.

It wasn't the world gone wrong, but something broke inside his head. He didn't think like normal people. Took pride in the fact; though he couldn't properly function in society; still he blamed everyone else.

He always expected something for nothing. As if the world owed him. He wanted the prize, but never wanted to play the game or follow the rules to attain it. He could tell a tale to break your heart for certain, but you never knew what was truth or lies. After a while it didn't matter. All the stories were the same. Different characters and scenes, but the premise never changed.

Deep seeded hatred for my family; resentful of our love, our normalcy, our faith and decency. They welcomed him in and he stood over and pissed on them. Just as he did me; time and time again.

My body bears the scars of our time together, though my heart and soul have properly mended. Ten years I spent with this man, seven as his wife. And the day I found the courage to leave, he pleaded and begged, pledged his devotion and love.

There is no devotion in a creature as such, nor do I believe, is there to be found any love. There will always be those who take pity, try to see the good for all the bad, the light despite the darkness; the wings bearing resemblance to those of an angel; but when your eyes finally open and you realize you're gazing into the face of the devil, it's often times too late.

But just as memories that fade with time, they eventually go away. Not because they don't want to stay; they feed off your emotion, your energy, your very life force if you will; but because they can't. Unable to settle, commit, connect with anything that is real. Blaming their surroundings; trapped and desperate for a way out. Running to be free, knowing in their heart they never will be. For the very thing they run from, dwells deep within them.

Wherever they go, they'll always be there. Their fate, their destiny; and a truth that brings comfort to those who suffered at their hand. That one day they will simply wallow to death in their own pathetic misery.

ETERNAL VALENTINE

It was a special year; more so than any they had ever shared. Having followed her to the dark side and come out alive; where he stood along the jagged edge, lifeline tightly secured, should she accidentally fall or simply choose to jump.

Taking the hits as she dished them out. Not once did he waiver, even when his mind overflowed with doubt; his heart filled with gut-wrenching pain. His love for her an anchor; keeping them tethered, so as not to drift any farther apart; into that raging sea of madness where illusion had her believing she belonged.

He is her strength in times of weakness; the rock upon which her foundation is built; the voice of reason in her moments of insanity; the path that guides when she loses her way; the beacon of light illuminating the darkness; the arms of tenderness that wrap round where she lays.

Loving her completely. Through it all. Beyond.
To the end. Back again...

Her Husband
Her Love
Her Partner
Her Friend

To my Valentine.

GRAND ILLUSION

He brought her deeper
Inside her Self

Revealing truth
As he thought he
Knew

Wanting to be her
Maker

Her own personal
Jesus

Filling her soul
Illusions of
Grandeur

Only one thing
She ever did
For him

Re-instilled the
Dream
Taking him
Farther
Away from
He

The only thing
He ever
Wanted

That place he
Longs to
Be

DEATH TRAP

She doesn't seek his memory, it just comes creeping; and when it does, that's all there is.

It's nothing to do with fear or inspiration; building a fan base that was there long before he was; or anything at all for matter of fact. For who would dream of seeking such hurt.

Its simply a means of soul survival; an attempt to heal, her wounds on her own. Purging her being in the form of words; bloodletting her system of his poison, his disease. Being caught in the death trap, he sets and springs.

His desperation for reprieve, amounting to nothing; empty words of apology and pleas of forgiveness. He gobbles her words and his ego grows, waiting for Twitter to tell him there's more.

AT THE BOTTOM OF THE WELL ...

...lies a pathetic creature of habit. So vile as to burn your eyes blind, should you cast your gaze upon him for too long a time. Haunted by demons of a horrific past, or a victim of sheer lunacy, telling tall tales; weaving colorful yarns, his mind simply mad.

I often wondered of his angst; whether it was genuine or completely contrived; the product of trying to emulate the lives of those great minds whose books he consumed – not once, nor even twice, but endless, countless times; as a drunkard takes to wine; believing to have glimpsed his soul, on the yellowed crumpled pages, between the lines of others words.

Forever lost, questioning reality, obsessing over the meaning of existence and whether or not he's really here; leaving a trail of pain and tears in his wake; feeding off whatever scrap of emotion he can evoke and they willingly give; feasting on regret, as it's the only feeling strong enough to remind him he's alive.

ABSINTHE WISHES AND
LITHIUM DREAMS

He wanders aimlessly through worlds of destruction; mist colored mountains, too blinded to see. A victim of self-induced misfortune, an inflicter of pain. Endless. Eternal. Walking through the flames, wearing the scars like badges of honor; baptisms of fire consecrated in vain.

Infinite lifetimes spent. Second-hand knowledge attained. Wasted on this tortured mind; soul hollowed eons ago. A teacher to some perhaps, but no man of genius as once she believed. Prostituting his suffering for personal gain; unwilling to succumb to sanity's necessity.

Eager to believe his revelations; as if he, a mere mortal, born with transcendent faculties; innate knowledge awarded by God. A favored soul having lived a longer time. Acquired more. Progressed further. Ordained and reincarnated at the desire of God; to aide the progress of mankind; or at the very least, the twin of her flame; to continue the journey, on the path by her side.

A monster disguised as her own personal savior; a wanton demon, this King of the Damned. Driven now by the voice in his head, whispering night and day; pushing him further, closer to the edge. *"Burn the pages, take your bow; sweet surrender in dawns early hour."*

Fare thee well; to you, Dark Prince; on your voyage, your final affair. Role fulfilled, as it was written; take heed in the knowing; until we meet again…

U N I V E R S I T Y & U S 1

I sit in my car. Heat on, espresso hot, music soothing; and I'm bitching internally about the traffic; and on occasion, out loud, as someone in close proximity pulls some stupid stunt worthy of my expletives. And I ask myself; how is possible to leave fifteen minutes early, only to arrive at my destination twenty minutes late? Why do people in this town not know how to drive?!

There are laws, but very few abide by them. There are rules, but the majority make up their own as they go; whatever happens to suit their own personal need at the time. Forget common sense and courtesy; this is road war; every man for himself!

And as I reach for my piping hot espresso, which will soothe my soul and calm my nerves, I look over and see him. Body tense, shoulders hunched, back to the wind though it still pierces his flesh. And suddenly I am forced to reassess…

He arrives by the 1105 bus each morning at 5am sharp; where he makes his way to the center median of the busiest intersection in the city. He places his plastic milk crate at the end of the median. This is where he will stop, sit, and momentarily rest; when the ache in his legs shoots that fire-like pain up into his lower back and forces him to do so. He dons his neon green vest, and until that time he weaves his way in and out of traffic; timing the lights just right, so that he can take advantage of all four lanes.

I watch him in my mirror, hustling his newspapers; walking past car after car. The light turns green, the two turn lanes begin to move and he runs back to his post on the concrete median. I silently count my blessings, as he inhales deeply, puffs out his cheeks and expels a slow breath of frustration. In that moment I feel his pain; and I am ashamed.

Ashamed for all that I take for granted.
Ashamed that at times I seem ungrateful.
Ashamed that I'm drinking a $6 coffee and have no cash for a paper.

One o'clock rolls around. The traffic from lunch is beginning to die down. He picks up the remaining papers and carefully places them in his crate. He removes the lightweight canvas tool pouch from his waist, folds it carefully so as not to spill any of his earnings and sandwiches it between the unsold news. He's put in his 8 hours and earned almost $30. He's cold, tired, hungry; and ready to call it a day.

GRAZING AT THE CORRAL

It sits back off the main drag and the only time I ever notice it is when someone is in front of me turning in; inevitably I end up screaming, *"Turn the wheel already!"* as it seems to take for fucking ever for people to pull in that lot. Now granted, there's a bit of a downhill slope going in, but still, the entrance is plenty wide enough for two cars; so even if there's one waiting to get out there shouldn't be this problem. And that's another thing; on this particular drag, people usually jet out in front of you; kind of like the cat that decides to wait and bolt across the street until you're within squishing distance; but not here, not one time has a car ever pulled out in front of me, even when there was ample space to do so.

I've never given any of this much thought, until my son couldn't decided what he wanted for lunch the other day and suggested we go there, because the choices were limitless; the operative word here being limitless.

We pulled in and I was amazed at not only the size of the place, but of the ginormous parking lot! Normal parking lots barely give you enough space to park your car and open the doors to get out, but this one…this one was like something you see in the parks in Orlando; it seemingly stretched on forever.

We park. Fling our doors open wide. Head inside.

The first thing I notice are the announcements posted all over the outside windows beside the curiously wide automatic opening double-doors; announcing things like, "Kids Night," "Steak Night," "Fish Fry Friday," "Senior Sunday Special," and on and on and on…

We walk in and there before us is a roped-off lobby. Not just roped off mind you, but picture if you will, permanent wooden dividers that wind back-and-forth; the kind of like the line you patiently make your way through while waiting to get on a carnival ride; carnival being the operative word here…

Unbeknownst to us, we had entered the twilight zone of titillating taste temptation; the mecca of munching madness; the fantasy world of flesh-filling fabulous feasting; a pit stop for the gluttonous, where they can graze their way to purgatory. Yes…we were trapped in the bowels of the Golden corral.

Bud, the rotund assistant manager, as his shiny gold name tag proudly displayed, greeted Henrieta and Charlie, who were in line ahead of us; with a warm, friendly smile, as he informed them that their normal table appeared to be empty. We stepped up to the cash register, Bud welcomed us; making mention that he'd never seen us here before and was this our first visit; to which I shook my head and held onto my son's hand; looking back over my shoulder to see if there was any other way out but to run wildly through the maze.

There wasn't. We were trapped; and so I reached in my pocket and pulled out my money; a twenty, to which I received a large chunk of change back. I looked at the money in my hand, then back at Bud, with a devilish gleam in his eye and realized he was one of Satan's spawns; encouraging over-eating and giving the shit for free!

We got our drinks, found a table and made our way to the buffet. We chose wisely and even then didn't completely fill our plates; our appetites quickly dissolved as we diverted our eyes from our plates and dared to sneek a peek at the people that surrounded us.

A couple to the left; he with two chairs pushed together and still hanging over both sides and she in her wheelchair; belly hanging over the edge, seemingly dangling somewhere around her knees; although her knees could not be seen, so really, it was anyones guess.

Hundreds of busy worker bees, filling and refilling the food stations; clearing the contents of temporarily abandoned tables onto heavily laden trays, filling cups with pitchers of colorful drinks. A distraught little woman sweating over the grill; unable to keep up with the demand; announcing to all those who approached that the steaks would not be up for fifteen more minutes. Watching the big burly men hang their heads, pull down their caps and shuffle their way over to the chicken buffet instead. Fat little kids running wild; bowls heaped with ice cream and sprinkles; chocolate syrup smeared across their faces from previous trips to the desert island.

It was all just too much to bear!

We left without cleaning out plates, neither of us eating our $6 worth; ignoring Bud on the way out as he bid us a fond farewell and told us to come back again real soon. We ran to the van, jumped in and locked the doors behind us. Only then, when we were safe from the madness, did we vow never to return to the gates of Hell; known simply as the Golden Corral.

OBSERVATIONS (1)

outside my window…

a plethora of birds happily sing, while a light breeze blows warm on my skin. The Queen Palm stretches her frond, to caress the trunk of the mighty old oak; while the blue sky can be seen and beckons

between its branches. Somewhere a dog barks, far off in the distance. He doesn't sound happy; mine looks at me from her spot in the sun and asks what we're going to do today.

I can think of nothing so pressing as to require my time; or anything I'd rather do, than sit in quiet solitude, absorbing the magnificence of this glorious day. Counting my blessings, happy to be alive; no darkness, no demons, just perfection, peace and light…

IT DOESN'T TAKE MUCH

We were sitting at the light, side-by-side. Two little girls in the front seat of a minivan; seven and five if I had to guess. They were each brushing their hair, trying to share the mirror in the visor. I have no way of knowing how far they had traveled; sharing the front seat, playing at being girls; but I do know that they were completely unprotected.

I sat there watching, my blood pressure rising; attention shifting from the children to the mother; carefree oblivion filling the interior space; and I just wanted to roll down my window and scream; *What the fuck is wrong with you?!*

The little one got up and moved to the back and a minute later the one in the front closed the mirror and put on her seat belt. I'm not certain if she did this of her own volition, or her mother said something, but the little one, now in the back, sat sideways in her seat; brush in hand, looking at me through the tinted glass.

I watched her for a few minutes then gave the shoulder strap of my seatbelt a few little tugs and smiled back. She immediately turned forward in her seat and I watched as she pulled the belt around her, fastening it in place. She looked back to see if I was watching. I smiled and gave her thumbs up.

The last thing I saw before the light turned green and we went our separate ways, was her proud little smile spread from ear-to-ear, matching my own.

Bringing a child into the world does not automatically make you a parent. All I have to do is open my eyes and look around to be reminded of this every single day. However, once you reach that place, I believe once a mother, always a mother.

The fact that connection and communication was made; instruction given and taken; all without a single word spoken; not between two perfect strangers, but between a child and a parent, proves yet again, that it doesn't take much; just a mixture of caring, common sense and love.

BROKEN MIRROR

None of it matters
It was all just an illusion
My muse is simply snagged on a shadow
Working her way free…

LUAU OF LIFE

Turquoise Jesus
In all His
Holiness
Dangling transparent
From her rearview
Mirror

Surrounded by flowers
Tangerine
Tropical
Glued to the
Dash
A plastic girl
Giving hula

Finding false
Comfort
In her co-pilot and
Lucky charm

I wonder…

Does a silver plaque
Warn
Pinned to her visor
To never drive
Faster
Than your angel
Can fly

I'M LISTENING

The universe is calling; and I am listening. Ensnared in the trap for far too long; searching for a Sage while wallowing in angst. Conceding to the darkness as it consumed and controlled. Though not completely, and not any more.

The universe is whispering; and I am listening. Mother Nature opens her arms, enveloping me in her warm embrace; showing me beauty, nature's sanctuary; her peace, her bounty and all her glory.

The universe is beckoning; and I am following. A child of Aries, beginning anew; harnessing energy, strength and truth. Turning attention from outward to within, finding my Sage the moment I did.

DON'T KNOW WHY

She dies a little more
Each time
Following in the dark
A shadow drifting
Unnoticed

Across his frenzied life
Watching movements
As it unfolds
And still she wonders
With every word
He strokes

BORN ANEW

He forced her to look at the world, in a way she never had before. Bringing out the best in her, while dancing with the devil in her. Two people coming together, no matter the reason or cause; finding several common threads that held them together for a while.

When time had come for both to move on, perhaps it was easier to force feed her that bitter pill, rather than muster a proper goodbye; knowing if he didn't she'd hang on forever.

Perhaps.

In truth, the recovery took her to new depths of darkened despair, but in the end brought her nothing but good. For she was, in fact, born anew; in mind, body, spirit and soul. Forced to open her eyes and examine minutely, the reflection looking back from within the broken mirror.

Where without him she might be dwelling still, in that fog filled existence she once thought of as living.

STRANGE PEACE

The house was almost 200 years old when I lived there as a child; one of the oldest in the village. There were trees around it then; one in the corner where the small pine is now and one in the front, across from the porch. This one had a large bolder beside it that I used to climb and play on. We also had permanent awnings over all the windows if I recall. What I do recall, with perfect clarity, are the spirits with whom I dwelled.

The incidents varied, but occurred regularly. I spent most of my time living in a constant state of fear and terror. Though I never said anything to my mother until years after; when she verified that it wasn't simply my overactive imagination, by sharing her own experiences with me.

It didn't matter whether inside or out; they found me wherever I was. Although, if sent outside, I spent most of my time visiting with the old ladies that lived on the block; and while they {the spirits}, made their presence known to me, they never followed me out of the yard.

It was strange, my relationship with the ladies. There were three of them in all; Agnes, who lived two houses down, Mrs. McAdams who lived across the street and the lady behind us whose name I can't remember, but can see clearly the two large ferns that sat atop brass stands in her sitting area, and her two Pomeranians that looked like little foxes.

And while the candy in the porcelain dishes was usually stale, and lunch consisted of green onion and mayonnaise sandwiches, our conversations, on those occasions when we chose to talk, was typically a Q & A session about their lives. Normally this was prompted by a piece of jewelry or dress that I came out wearing; asking of the origin and when and where they had worn them.

They never minded that I rummaged and ransacked their closets, drawers and jewelry boxes, because I took them back; took them to a place that might not have been forgotten, but was rarely, if ever, spoken of. They told their stories, with far away looks in their eyes and I listened intently; while sipping bitter tea from china cups and eating my onion-mayo finger sandwiches with the crust neatly trimmed off.

These were peaceful times for me, when the majority of my world consisted of things that were beyond my comprehension; beyond this world entirely. But there were a few times when I was sent to my room {far right window – second floor}, for whatever reason, and it was everything I could do to hold my eyes open. I distinctly remember the cross breeze blowing in over me, as I lay on top of my bed; the sweet scent of lilacs wafting in with it, bringing a smile that filled me with happy, from the inside out; and a gentle caress along my head and back, which brought me strange peace and comfort incomparable to any I had ever known.

It was as if God Himself were lulling me to sleep; which was completely understandable in my mind, as He lived right across the street in the church that sat on the opposite corner. When I wasn't with the ladies, I was playing on the front steps of the church; knowing full well that not only could they not get me there, but didn't even dare show themselves!

Yesterday I was at a loss; unable to find the words to adequately describe the beauty of the day, which filled and overwhelmed me completely. Suddenly, it was all I could do to keep my eyes open. All was quiet, but for the breeze rustling in the trees; the southern sun warming the earth around me. I had done everything that needed doing and found myself lying atop my bed; the gentle breeze blowing over me, as I lay gazing at the moss swaying in the treetops, and suddenly I was taken back; to a place that has never been forgotten, but is rarely, if ever, spoken of.

I could feel the shift the moment it happened; the temperature of the breeze changing dramatically, the heady scent of lilacs filling my senses, though there are none in this area; and a gentle, familiar caress along my head and back; filling me with that same strange peace that I hadn't felt in some thirty odd years.

I was taken back to be reminded; but reminded of what?

That the demons I've wrestled of late are of my own creation and insignificant in comparison to those I faced in the past? That although we may dwell alongside demons, of human and spirit origin, He is right across the street and watching always?

I pondered the reasons, briefly; as I closed my eyes and allowed my self to be lulled to sleep…

BOULEVARD OF THE BIZARRE

It's like an alternate universe
One that makes my skin crawl
Though I know it shouldn't
Still I can't help my self

Littered with the dregs of society
And side show carnival freaks
Where the Twilight Zone meets the Dark Side
It's the Boulevard of the Bizarre

Don't know where they come from
Where they're going
Where they've been
Diseased crack whores on every corner
Physically deformed driving wheelchairs like cars

Mentally disabled talking to street signs
Blind men hanging onto bus stop posts
Doctors behind the wheels of Mercedes'
Staring blindly straight ahead

Maneuvering to my destination
Trying desperately not to cringe
I know I shouldn't feel this way
But somehow I can't help my self

What if one of them were Jesus
Or all in the image of Him
Is this really someone I want to meet
Are these thoughts considered sin

OBSERVATIONS (2)

I wonder sometimes
If people even know
The length and width
Of their modes of
Transportation

And just how close
They often come
While jetting in and out
Obliviously blind

To taking lives

FADED SCARS

I feel for her.
Sort of.
Maybe not so much.
I want to warn her.
Sometimes.
Never mind.
Let her learn the hard way.
Would do no good anyway.
Earn her badge among the ranks.
Ugly scars like the rest of us wear.
Or rather wore, I should say.
Mine are gone now.
How about yours?

ADDICTION

The sound of beans grinding
The smell of fresh ground roasting
Espresso machines espressing
White cups overflowing

Thick black boldness
Life sustaining liquid
Reddish-brown foam
Proper known as crema

Never ending circle
Black green and white
Crowned Siren at its center
The eternal symbol of goodness

A beacon of comfort
In the storm of life
Warmth for the soul
In a world gone awry

LETTER TO OPHELIA

Dearest Ophelia,

It has been so long since we sat and talked. There once was a time; long, long ago, when there was nothing we didn't share. Two young girls; hearts brimming with hopes, dreams and silly fears, of that which was unknown; much that we only imagined, some truths that even now are difficult to comprehend; but still, here we are; all these years later, reaching out and connecting. Confidences shared, vulnerabilities exposed, trusts forged; and life goes on.

I must confess that I often miss those days of youthful innocence, but treasure the memory of them always. And so it was with abundant respect that I accepted your news of this second chance of which you spoke; with such heartfelt joy that it leapt from the page and struck my own soul.

For I too know about second chances, am well versed in affairs of the heart; and can tell you with complete and utter certainty that soul mates and twin flames do, indeed, exist.

Your happiness is such that you spend every waking moment in a state of euphoria; counting the moments until you can be together again. The wait is agony, yet such sweet suffering it is; for you know what awaits you and how far you have traveled to finally meet at this crossroad once more.

There are times when you fight sleep; unable to bear the pain of such missing, during your hours of slumber; and at others, you cannot wait to rest your head, close your eyes with the memory of him fresh in your mind, the scent of him still lingering; recounting every second spent, ever word spoken, every touch and caress; given and felt; knowing full well that you will find him in your dreams.

Ah, yes, how well I know this love you speak of. Having rejoiced and basked in its eternal promise; suffered and sacrificed to attain that which I needed more than my next breath. Knowing full well that should it ever cease to exist, so would life as I had come to know it. The pain, the torment, the agony and the angst; diffused completely by a single embrace.

But I warn you, dearest Ophelia, that second chances are not for the faint of heart. Most will never know the meaning of true love; cannot fathom that somewhere on this earth there is a twin that completes and makes us whole. And so, if a second chance, by fates hand be granted, you must grasp it with every ounce of your being and be mindful to wrap with ties that bind, but never constrict.

There will be those who scoff and scorn; will bring up past mistakes; of yours, his and those you made together, when the ignorance of youth was all you knew and held you under its wicked spell. Know that such negativity is not given out of love, but is born of pure, unadulterated jealousy. Resentful and loathing of you, are they; because you have found and accepted that which they know not the meaning of.

Take heed, Ophelia, when I tell you that there are those who would rather see you suffer as they, than rejoice and share in your happiness. They may not even be consciously aware of their actions; and so it is up to you to proceed with eyes wide open; armed and ready, to battle for that which your heart does know.

I leave you with my blessing and full support. Go now, to the man of your dreams; the keeper of the key, that fits the lock you fastened tightly around your heart. Trust your intuition, your inner voice; make every moment count and live your life with him well.

In light,
Anastasia

EMOTION IN MOTION

Fourteen hours of endless highway
Thoughts ticking down the miles
The journey is over
Darkness calls
Spirit settles
I am done...

ILLUSION

She believed
From the beginning
That he
Was the one

He knew all along
She was just
One
Of many

TAILLIGHTS DISSOLVE

Nineteen hundred
Eighty seven
Miles
On the road
Slaying ghosts

A PATH WITH HEART

Standing on the edge
Looking on
Dark shadows shroud
The path

Those who would happily
Drag me down
Waiting to take
My hand

Following for a
While
Truth revealing itself
In darkened halls
I do not wish
To dwell

For though at
Times
My soul grows
Weary
Darkness offering
Such sweet embrace

My heart overflows
This blinding
Light
I no longer
Can deny

LOST IN THE FAÇADE

I told him once he was a praise whore, and thought he was going to cry. The look of hurt shown in his eyes nearly broke my heart.

But still, what I said was truth.

I tried to reach that part of him; beyond the shallows, into the depths, and for a moment successfully glimpsed. But it didn't last long; nothing discussed apparently took. For he's still just as shallow, if not more so; worrying what the rest of the world thinks; determining his human worth by the number of possessions he can acquire, the number of heads he can turn, and how many times he stands at center of attention.

Trying so very hard to impress; bragging as a child might, as if to say, "Look what I have and you don't," when of all the people in the whole of the world, he knows I'm the queen of modest living and that material possessions of any kind, simply do not impress.

I wouldn't be on the receiving end of his karma for all the money in the world! And what strikes me as odd, is that after all this time and distance, why he goes out of his way, to make certain that I see?

He should ask himself that at night, when he lays his head on his designer pillow, next to his lunatic wife, convincing himself that he's finally made it, and happiness he has found.

UTOPIA

River bottom
Dwellers
Got the muddy water
Blues

OVATION

She waits
Wonders
Pines
For love lost

Just as we
All did

The same
Love
The same
Lies
Differing his pain
His troubled past

To fit each
Woman
And circumstance

Depending
On what he
Needed
Or knew he could
Take from them

I offered up the
Group of support
Gathered in the
Wings

Patiently waiting
For her to
Walk off the
Stage

She isn't yet
Ready
Still believing
He is
Who he
Says

LETTER TO VERONICA

Dear Veronica Lake,

The truth of us.

Something you believe only the two of you share; yet something we've all been forced to wonder about. We too had a truth in an airport, he and I; just as he had truths made up of lies with a plethora of intelligent, creative, beautiful, loving, soulful women; all of which were spoon-fed the exact same line, differing only slightly, as the situation, circumstance and female heart warranted.

At this point, you refuse to believe that which your mind has forced you to wonder of; as your heart precariously dangles by a soul string. Wanting so much to believe that he is who he says, that YOU are the twin of his flame, the mate of his soul and yours is the only connection that is real and matters. Refusing to believe that what you shared during your time together meant nothing, when it meant and still means, absolutely everything to you.

Finally realizing, for the first time in your life, since your karmic connection, that YASS, this is the way it was intended. Finally another soul on earth, who understands you like none other. No judgments; just complete, unconditional acceptance and love. Exactly what you always knew, in the depths of your soul, love was supposed to be. Every wasted moment and past mistake leading to this crossroad that brought the two of you together....

Ignoring the red flags, due to his lifetime membership within the upper echelons of intelligencia. Stories of his dysfunctional and abusive childhood, which as a mother you can surely sympathize. His self-destructive pain and angst, leading him to long for death; his only comfort found within darkness' welcome embrace; singing always that sweet song of stygian.

Believing in your heart that your love for him can and will make a difference; that happiness can be found and shared, if only he would allow himself to trust, believe and take your hand. At this point, your perception of your own reality so skewed that you know for certain the only way to survive this life is with him by your side.

Wake up, love. This isn't a classic movie you're starring in; this is your life you're allowing him to fuck with. There's an antidote for those of us who have been infected with this disease; the first step is realizing you want and need to be cured.

The sooner you realize that there is no truth where the Hyena is concerned and the only reason he will ever come back is if there is something he needs from you, which he cannot provide for himself; the better off you and yours will be.

The only way to get back to living is by killing the Hyena. He must become dead to you in order to see and accept the truth; the only truth there is of him. The one too many of us have come to know…

REFLECTIONS IN DREAMS

My dreams took me back last night; to a place I haven't been in over a decade; a place I never imagined my self being, and never want to be again.

Ten years devoted.
Ten years spent.
Irretrievable.
Broken.
Gone forever.

I entered through the familiar front door; the scent that was us overwhelmed and stopped me in my tracks. My eyes adjusted then focused in the dark, as familiar images and shapes appeared before me. I slowly walked from room to room; each containing different objects from various stages of our time together.

Our first living room, with hand-me-down sofa and chair; knick-knacks and pictures, arranged just as they had been. Even the flowers I'd picked from the field; beginning to dry, yet colorful in the blue glass vase.

I walked down the hall and another room appeared; another chapter displayed for my viewing. More of his things mingled with mine; his presence now obvious and prominent. The same wildflowers, faded now, but still beautiful through my eyes; the blue glass vase, a crack now in its side, simply added character, I remember thinking.

There was an entryway that led to a carport; our Tibetan Mastiffs, Marge & Homer, who I secretly called Rhett & Scarlett, obediently on their cushion in the corner. Both in dire need of baths and a nutritious meal; something other than what happened to be on sale. Scarlett looked up at me with those pitiful, sad eyes; as if to ask me why; the single word and loaded question that plagued me at the time; plagued us all. Rhett refusing to acknowledge me; having long since given up on me; that day I lay on the bathroom floor; Scarlett faithfully curled by my side, offering unconditional love and support; while Rhett stood looking from the door, his gaze as if to say, "who's the coward now?"

There were boxes stacked to the ceiling in the far corner of the carport; waiting to be stored in the attic; something he always promised he was going to get to, but never did. For the simple fact that they contained my things; things I took with me wherever we happened to land; things that were sentimental, things he felt threatened by. And so they sat in that corner, exposed to the elements, until they finally began rotting away.

I remember the day I drug them to the curb on garbage day; one by one. I didn't even have the heart to go through them; to be reminded of what they contained; to see what treasured possessions had been ruined and lost to me forever. Better to not remember, I told my self.

I walked back inside; looked to my left, then to my right; trying to decide which way to go; how to get out. There was no easy way; not then, not even in my dreams. There was, however, a light at the end of a long, dark hall; which I instinctively moved toward. As I progressed, I passed many more rooms. Some of which I stopped, stood in the doorway of, and gazed at with fond reminiscence; others I rushed past, with nothing more than a glance given. And that one in particular that I would have expected to run right past, I actually stepped into.

I stood just inside the doorway, the light at the end of the hall beckoning, as the scene before me ripped my heart apart; piece by broken piece. Framed works of art that once I had been so proud, hung in precarious positions throughout the room; not out of eclecticism, but sheer necessity; covering holes that had been punched, kicked or gouged in the walls. Markers of his anger, reminders of his horrible temper; hidden in plain sight.

Neon beer signs and alien figurines still made me cringe, and not a single book in sight, for that was nothing but a ridiculous waste of time. The stench of the homemade bong on the table in the corner; my good lemonade pitcher with a bottomless 2-liter bottle stuck inside; brown water and thick repugnant ganja residue covering the sides. The sound he made as he inhaled two full liters of smoke into his lungs, and the desperation in his eyes when he was forced to scrape the sides. The bong disappearing, new paraphernalia taking it's place; diverting my gaze before the crack pipe and gun materialized.

I looked away, and there on the floor, in the corner by the loveseat, was my favorite Tommy Bahama bag. I walked over and picked it up, slowly unzipped it and looked inside. A half smoked pack of Marlboro Lights, a black and white composition book that I used for a journal back then; half the pages ripped out and the remaining filled with written lies to appease his insecure ego and get him the fuck off my back; little doodles on the pages, where he had left his mark, his way of letting me know he had been there, read my words and that nothing of mine would ever be sacred.

I removed the sparkly silver Lancome make-up bag my mother had sent me, pulled out the compact and opened the secret compartment in the bottom; and there it was, the light at the end of the tunnel; shining brightly in my hand, just as it always had done. I carefully removed the small, aged piece of paper and unfolded it, to reveal the message inside that had kept me sane, given me courage and one day eventually saved my life, quite literally.

"I'll Love You Forever…"

I carefully refolded the note, but instead of putting it back where I'd found it, I slipped it in my pocket; thinking to myself, that he really does and undoubtedly will…love me forever. Just then I felt his arm slip comfortably around my waist. I turned to look and there he was; my beautiful husband, standing by my side, where he'd been all along, right from the start. I looked deep, into his smiling eyes; filled with happiness and love that would never be disguised.

We were silent for several minutes, as we stood in the doorway and gazed about the room. Remembering those tumultuous years when we'd only just met, the insanity I was living through and his desire to help. I spotted the small pottery bowl I'd made when I was a little girl; musing that it had actually survived. It's pink, purple and blue hues faded with time. I walked over and retrieved it from its spot of safety, and inside lay the broken shards of my blue glass vase; that I didn't have the heart to throw away, that was still beautiful, even in pieces, through my eyes.

I handed it to him, but the only thing he saw when he looked inside, were remnants of a broken heart, a shattered soul; in desperate need of healing, and he the one to do the mending; still beautiful, even when broken, through his eyes.

When I woke from the dream I found him curled at my back; two spoons in a drawer, with his arm around my waist. Offering comfort, with me always. Weathering life's storms and the changing of the seasons.

SEPARATE REALITY

The music strikes a cord, as rain falls steady outside your four doors; and you feel him suddenly, tugging at your soul. Memories come down like raindrops on the windshield; and you realize with gripping certainty, just how close you came to throwing it all away; for a stranger whose specialty was manipulating words; who didn't just consume, but devoured every morsel; your heart, your soul, your poetry and prose; digging your mind, inspiring your muse, feigning a connection while loving your soul…

MR EUGINE

Born in the North, I often dreamed of the South; when I did, images were conjured of grand old plantation estates, with wrap around porches and marble columns visible from the end of long oak-lined lanes; branches canopying the way, silver-grey moss swaying in the sultry southern breeze; thick with the heady scent of magnolia.

And these trees, these Magnolias, like none other I'd ever seen. As if a southern gentleman, in every respect; grand and prominent in stature, strong and virile; dressed out in the finest leaves; waxy green, thick like leather, commanding attention amongst all others. Then true to form, offering up a bouquet of simple, yet elegant blossoms that fill the air with a decadent perfume that can be detected for miles around.

How I love the south; with her abundance of beautiful offerings; as if the birthplace of Mother Nature herself.

And then one day, during my exploration, I ventured a little deeper, walked a little further; past the tall white, stately mansions, stumbling quite by accident, upon rows of little shacks; where the beauty faded and her ugly truth was revealed; slapped hard in the face with reality; which left a scar on my heart that will always remain; stinging pain forever to be felt. As I gazed at the torturous device, the post erected for lashings. I could hear the screams that pierced the night, the crack of the bullwhip wielded by that prominent plantation master; stripped of his gentlemanly façade, a brutal racist torturer taking his place.

Everything was suddenly perfectly clear; as I gazed at the giant old oaks and magnolias I stood among; their natural beauty still visible through my eyes, yet I couldn't help but wonder of the deadly secrets that might be told; the brutal sins in which they were forced to assist. The south has never been the same to me since.

And so one day, while browsing an antique shoppe, nestled among Civil War era memorabilia, I saw this saintly little man staring down at me. My instincts told me how wrong it was, that his creation had been forged from controversy and for all the wrong reasons. But right or wrong, I had to have him. I had to take him out of that place and give him a home where he would be revered, respected, admired and cherished; the truth of his history never forgotten, his story retold to any who asked, and all who would listen.

I call him Mr. Eugine, and his home is a permanent spot on my desk. He's become my talisman, my inspiration, my symbol of hope, and my muse on days like this. His presence humbles me, keeps me thankful, and quite simply makes me smile. And so on this day, when that stately gentleman  I call the magnolia, offers up his first heady bouquet to me, I pick a single blossom and bring it home as my own offering. An offering of forgiveness, in memory and in honor of all those who suffered and lost their lives on the very soil I now tread and dwell, this place I call my home. This place I proudly share with Mr. Eugine; for all the right reasons.

PROCESSING AND PURGING

Hearing the truth
The ugly truth
Trying hard to process
What it really means

Was always a bitter pill
But somehow easier to swallow
At least when there was something
A reason on which to blame

Delusional
Madness
Insanity
Lunacy

An innate inability
To deal
To cope
To live
To feel

A falsity I now
Am forced to ingest
For the veil has been lifted
On his façade of mental illness

GOES THE LIGHT

Comes the darkness
Raindrops fall
Shards of glass
Shred the soul

Storm moves out
Waters calm
Gripping numbness
Seize the heart

INSANITY'S FINAL ADIEU

His was a miserable life; wandering the globe pretending to be lost, feigning insanity due to all sorts of abuse; self-inflicted, youthful demons victim, to any and all who showed the slightest inclination of interest. In truth, he knew exactly where he was going, what the cost would be to get there; needing only to cross paths with enough unsuspecting souls to help him reach his final goal.

His mantra; a worn out stanza touting suicidal tendencies, despair and angst; deviously reaching out, spewing his seed deep into the core of one vulnerable victim after another. Setting his life on cruise control; riding the tides at the expense of others; completely void of moral conscience. Reveling in his cunning; laughing yass…Yass…YASS!!!

Glorifying and romanticizing his untimely demise; misunderstood soul, plagued to the point of suicide; lamented by the masses, singing his praises; his spirit rising, watching from above. Egomaniac, if ever there was. Imagining himself, even in death; the center of attention, in the form of ash.

What he didn't equate in the miles obsessively tracked, was the road itself reaching up; in the cloak of darkness, snatching his pathetic ass. There would be no bright light, no tunnel of peace; only a blazing ball of fire, an eternity of scorching heat.

The spell broken at the moment of death; his pact with the devil signed and sealed; damaged souls once broken, now healed. A fitting adieu; to one who once declared that Karma is but a word…

SOME TIMES

Sometimes I just
Want to scream
The truth of others
Too much to take

Zero tolerance
Lack of character
Human ignorance
Me mentality

People spewing
Meaningless words
No forethought
No consideration
To consequential results

Self-centered nature
Tunnel vision
Unable to see
Beyond themselves

LIFE'S REVOLVING DOOR

Sitting for hours
Head full of foils
Watching in boredom
The continuous revolving door

A plethora of aged women
All come to get
Their hair done

Most of them there
Simply for cuts

One sassy dame
Opting for color
Burgundy streaks
In her thick
Silver mane

While others received
Their weekly roll

What struck me
Straightaway
Was their sense
Of style

Prominently reflected
In their choice of
Youthful clothes

So deeply that
I watched
In quiet fascination
Looking beyond
What time had
Done

With a shift of
Perception
Their spirits shown
Through

Time elapsed
In reverse

Until one-by-one
Young women
Emerged

I couldn't help
But wonder
As I gazed at
My own
Reflection

How I will be
Perceived
Once old age
Claims me

MEMORY HOLES

My mission was clear, determined in the hours preceding my slumber. A journey must be made in order to obtain the necessary information to formulate my plot. And so under the cloak of darkness, when my body and mind were at rest and the door to world's unknown lay open and waiting, my spirit took flight and magically passed through.

Preparation of meditation and cleansing are no longer necessary for me, as once they were. I simply bring to the forefront of my thinking that a journey is required, and once I reach a plateau of unconsciousness where my spirit is able to detach itself, it does so eagerly and without pause. As if triggering a mechanism, all that I see, hear, feel, taste and touch are recorded in the memory banks of my mind; for future extraction upon reentry of my spirit.

Astral flight, astral projection, out-of-body experience; call it what you will, the process is the same, though the outcome widely varies. Normally, there is a clear and decisive reason for these journeys; as the answer to a question or solution to a problem is sought. This time, however, I left myself wide open with no particular question or problem, just the need and want to visit a dimension I had never before traveled, in order to capture and create from whence I had come.

I was not disappointed, but I was however distressed and somewhat traumatized by the experience. It was as if I was being led, instead of traveling of my own free will, and the one doing the leading had a specific reason for taking me there. The reason was to reacquaint me with my sin. The destination was HELL!

The corridor was long and dark, with hard-packed dirt floors and walls of rock that were high and arched; like the tunnels they dig through mountains, only there was no end in sight.

As I was led through the center of the tunnel, glass-fronted rooms lined either side. In each room, or life-size box as I came to think of them, was a specific scene from my life; scenes of sin that I had forced myself to forget; filing them away in the deepest recesses of my mind, where I was certain they would stay locked. Suddenly, and without warning, forced to relive each and every one.

To stand outside the box and watch, grateful when the show was over and the box went dark; only to turn and see the miles and miles of sin that lay ahead; sin that I must now suffer; as no thought, regard or consideration was given at the time.

The dread I felt, at the prospect of having to suffer so many, pales in comparison to the shame, regret and repulsion I felt; as I watched myself commit one deadly sin after another.

I begged for mercy, but mercy was not given; for this is death at its inception and what each and every one of us must go through. While the decision has already been made, the process by which it was determined is played out for us; right before our eyes, in the form of our lives.

"Be certain that your sins will find you out."
Numbers 32:23

HE LEFT HER

He left her hanging
A Monet with no River Seine

He left her barren
An open book with no pages

He left her questioning
A riddle with no answer

He left her doubting
The truth of her very existence

He left her incomplete
Energy work only half started

He left her drowning
Gasping for breath within his mire

He left her broken
To sift the pieces of her shattered soul

He left her knowing
Demons walk among us in this material world

He left her prepared for battle
Should the next life find their souls colliding

He left her without warning
An illusion within his own

WORD OF THE DAY

One could safely say that the foundation of my world is built on words. More than mere combinations of letters that form individual, miscellaneous words; but rather thought-filled, provoking, emotion-packed messages; extracted from the depths of my soul; each exuding the essence of my very being.

In the past nine years, since I began writing professionally, I have touched the lives of countless people I have never met, people I will never know; forging a connection over time and distance, sharing the common thread that is this human experience; the basic nature of our current existence.

I have received multiple literary awards for my fiction and poetry; awards I am extremely proud of, but at the time believed I was not worthy of; this appreciation has come with experience and maturity; and in the realization that by casting my soul into the universe in the form of words, I can leave my own personal mark; an endless mark that ripples into infinity.

I am more than the title of my current position, more than the words that make up my name suggest, more than my family sees me as, more than most people will ever take the time to come to know. I do not base my worth on material possessions, the number of books that I sell, or my yearly income.

I am a spiritual being, living a temporary human existence. I know for certain that life continues after the body ceases to function and perishes. I also have a keen sense of the duality of good and evil that lurks in the soul of every human being. A gift that I once considered a curse; of seeing through the façade, and past the veil that reveals the true nature of the human soul.

In all my years of living and experience, it never ceases to amaze, the unsuspecting packages in which wickedness is disguised. The innocence that orchestrates the deception and the insecurity that drives it all.

My word of the day is Slander. One that holds powerful meaning with devastating consequences. One in which I believe some could benefit by acquainting themselves more intimately with…

Slander
/slændər/   slan☐der [slan-der] –
noun
1. defamation; calumny: rumors full of slander.
2. a malicious, false, and defamatory statement or report: a slander against his good name.
3. Law. defamation by oral utterance rather than by writing, pictures, etc.

–verb (used with object) 4. to utter slander against; defame.
–verb (used without object) 5. to utter or circulate slander.

INTERNAL HARD DRIVE

Something about that
Penetrating gaze
Of his

As if
He's looking
Right through

Studying the
Surface
Reading the
Expression

While searching
The cause
Within

Snickering at
The display
Emotions painted
On face

Knowing
What lingers
Inside

Certain of
Himself

Too much so
Some times

Just smile
And nod
Let it go

He strolls
In and out
Watching the
Show

Flowing like
Water
A river to
The sea

The Zen in
My path
In a place
Gone mad

Sunshine
That lights
Those dark
Days

OBSERVING LIFE

She turned the corner and pulled into the only available parking space, due to the church crowd descending on Starbucks after their weekly worship service. The line wrapped through the café and ended at the back door. She stood there in her acid wash jeans, tie-dye shirt and flip flops, lost in a sea of suits and floral spring dresses; visualizing the sign that hangs on her back gate "Hippies use side door," feeling a sinner in a roomful of saints. Yeah, right!

For years she did the organized religion thing and found herself completely disillusioned by the illusion, and so she happily became a solitary practitioner, concentrating on her own personal relationship with our maker and her place within the universe. Lately though, she'd been second-guessing herself and wondering of the choices she'd made; brought on entirely by the perceptions and misconceptions of others; a dangerous and wicked spell to fall asunder.

Similar to Isaiah 24:19 – *The earth is broken asunder. The earth is split through. The earth is shaken violently.* So too had her world become; feeling helpless and weak, to a situation in which she had no control, she found herself succumbing to the darkness where recently there had been only light.

It wasn't until she found herself deep in the well of solicitude, that she was reacquainted with her true self; shown the brightness of her own light that dwells inside. Reminded that no matter how black the darkness descends, how hopeless a situations seems, how hard one is slapped with adversity, the solution lies not always in reaching out to others for help, but by reaching deep, to the core of our very being and drawing from the never-ending reserves of strength of which we have been equipped.

A certainty she has learned from life experience. Something she was never taught in the sanctuary of a church. And so in that sea of suits and spring dresses, the hippie-chick took her place in line; shoulders squared, head up proud, and a knowing smile shining bright on her face; the sting of recent adversity fading fast.

THROUGH MY EYES

And still I stop and pause; capturing images such as this, when presented before my eyes; wondering always, if God truly dwells there…

EMPTY VESSEL

He stole away
Under the cloak
Of darkness

Backpack thrown
Carelessly
Over weary hunched
Shoulders

Filled with
Unsuspecting
souls
Carelessly collected
Over nowhere
Miles

Casting shadows
Of doubt
Calling it love
Leaving a trail
Of broken bits
Wherever he goes

SAVING GRACE

She was waiting for him when he got there, bruises on face, bundle in tow. He didn't recognize her. Why would he? She was just one of many. Nameless, faceless, irresponsible wenches; whose babies he'd single-handedly managed to save. Each representing a jewel in the crown that Christ would one day bestow upon him.

He strategically positioned his signs; alongside the road at the entrance of the driveway, where passersby could view, as well as anyone come seeking services. He was particularly proud of his newest acquisition; a six foot mini-billboard, sporting a larger-than-life African American toddler; holding a toy in one hand, a smile that would melt the hardest of hearts and a message that read simply – "I was Saved from Death by Adoption"

She stepped forward, arms outstretched in offering. "You gotta take her cause I can't keep her." He looked at her strangely, "Pardon me?" She quickly looked down into the sleeping face; wrapped in the pink and white stripped blanket they'd sent her home with from the hospital, then back at him.

"My mama done kicked me out and my boyfriend beat my ass. You told me everything would be alright; when I came here that day to get rid of it. But everything ain't alright!" He looked at her dumbfounded, "Surely you don't mean me to…."

"Listen mister, you stuck your nose in my business without being asked. You preached a good sermon of guilt when my mind was made up. I done knew the day I came here that I couldn't raise no baby. I ain't got no job and now I ain't even got no place to live."

He reached in his bag and pulled out a pamphlet; the same one he'd given her that day; listing all her available options along with several choice Bible verses, threatening hellfire and damnation."Here, take this. There's a number on the back you can call for special services."

She shook her head and thrust the baby into his arms, "I used all the money I had on bus fare to get here. I ain't got a phone even if I wanted to call. I got nothin…don't you get that?!"

The baby started to cry. His eyes grew wide with fear and his hands began to tremble. He started to protest; something he'd been doing publicly for the past fifteen years; but she was having no more of it.

"You wanna help? You wanna stand here and judge people when you don't know nothin about their life or what brought 'em here in the first place? You gonna stand here and pretend to care; claimin you're doin the work of the Lord? Then you best be ready to back up that claim! You cared for this baby enough to save from death when she was in my belly, well now she's here and she ain't got no one *that can* care for her. No one but you!"

She didn't wait for a response, but quickly turned and ran up the street, got to the corner and vanished from sight; leaving him with an unwanted child and choices to ponder; none of which he asked for, and none that would come easy.

4 : 4 4

4:44 eyes open wide
Lay in the dark
Gaze at the clock

4:44 make a wish
So the final chapter
Begins

4:44 everywhere I look
Is it malicious intent
Or only mere coincidence

4:44 how to break the spell
Locate and remove the
Emotional connection chip

4:44 she looked at his photo
Saw right through
Called his emotional baggage

4:44 he died that day
Sexual abuse at such
A young age

4:44 he lost all trust
Made it his life's mission
To punish all women

4:44 he took what he wanted
Truth of it was
I could have loved him

4:44 heartless son of a bitch
Died twice on my watch
Come to raise the dead

4:44 just go away
To your charm once more
I refuse to fall prey

STALKER STELLA

She asks questions
Too many
For my zone
Of comfort

Personal in nature
A stalkers arsenal
As if to glimpse
Inside my world

Ridiculous assumptions
Personal judgments
Strange fascination
Prying curiosity

Gathering information
Painting a picture
By what she sees
Thinks she knows

What is the purpose
This strange fascination
Just take my order
Give me my espresso

SEEKING TRUTH

Before the fire
Flames dancing bright
Quest for visions
Sought this night

SHALLOW SAL

Just as it began
To materialize
For the first time in
His life

Wrapping his head
His heart around it
Embracing with wild
Abandon

Shifting perception
To a clearer view
Uninhibited
Filled with wonder

Unveiling calm
In the storm of
His life
To his true self
Introductions made

Freedom offered
At too high a cost
He weighed the options
Too much to be lost

He fabricated a story
That fit the bill
Sold his soul
For that house on
The hill

Building his arsenal
Of material possessions
At the end of day
Believing he's
Made it

WORTH RETRIEVING

She watches the water
Flow lazily by her window
Gently being pulled
By the slow moving current

Offering further proof
In the power of connections
Something she once put
Total faith in

Reduced to a place
Where she no longer believes
Still searching for her own truth
Once given so freely

A journey she must make
In order to retrieve it
Tangled in that web
Of lies and deceit

REPARATION

Within her circle of stones
She drifts back to that place
Casting out shadows
Demons handsome face

Once lost in his darkness
A labyrinth of despair
Longing for an illusion
Twin flames sweet embrace

That lone wandering drifter
Disguised as a sage
Stealing souls
Trying to make it pay

She felt he was coming
Hyena slowly circling
Hell fires burning
Raging like lightening

Call down the thunder
Glance back courageously
Lifetimes spent stalking
Doors opening and closing

Atonement is sought
Peace offered up
Discounting her wrath
Holding nothing from the past

WASTED YOUTH

The parking lot was full
Spilling over onto the boulevard
Hearse at the ready
To lead the procession

102 in the shade
Suffocating humidity
No breeze to speak of
All those gathered
Dressed in black

Mourning the loss
Young life wasted
Blood and tears pouring
Tragically taken

Listening through the wall
Razors trembling fingers
As her mother fucked
Yet another unknown stranger

The warning signs
Flashing neon
Young voice hoarse
Screaming out for help

But she had no interest
In playing mother

Too busy living
Her own lost youth

The belle of the ball
Life's ongoing party
Of superficial friends
Hookups and hangovers

Standing at the graveside
Pounding in her head
Fist full of dirt
Her only child dead

ONE STEP BEYOND

Finding the capacity
To bend without
Breaking

A willingness to
Change
Or be changed

Some times
Often times
Easier said than
Done

REAP AND SOW

She was relaxing on the sofa, her mind slowly unwinding, from a week of insurmountable stress; nothing compared to what the following promised; still, trying hard not to think about it. Hoping for a reprieve; an escape perhaps. Two days with no alarms, no schedules to speak of, maybe if she was lucky, get a little time away. When he walked in the back door, she just sat there and stared. Wondering how long his mid-life motorcycle crisis was actually going to last.

"Who are you?" she heard the words escape her mouth; before her thoughts had a chance to register and stop her. His thick mane of hair, now silver like tinsel, fell casually over his shoulders. Stone wash jeans, slashed stylishly below the pockets; not purchased purposely, but naturally worn till the fabric frayed. Black tank top advertising the biker bar; obviously new, as she'd never before seen it; showing off his brown-as-a-biscuit tan, with that Native American tint of red. Her red man. Her Indian. A perfectly beautiful, unknown stranger.

"I'm your man," he answered with certainty; swaggering confidently to where she sat on the sofa, "Come home to my baby." She turned her head when he bent down to kiss her. Not sure why, not thinking about it twice. Uncertainty filling her mind, taking hold of her senses. Tears threatening to spill over, fighting hard to hold them back; disguise her true feelings, whatever the cost.

The gift of deception, wrapped in a pretty pink bow; always the one she gave unsuspectingly; coming back to haunt her, every bit of three-fold. Not what she asked for, but exactly what she deserves. That old bitch Karma, lingering in the wings...

COLLECTIVE FEAR

I feared the words
He spoke were truth

Of me
About me
In spite of me

Because
He knew me

Because
I let him

Because
I wanted him to

Like none other
Before or after

Deeper
Better

To the core

Then left to wonder
If he knew me
At all

ALWAYS THE WHY

Why is it
So much easier

To hate him

Than try to
Understand

Why he did it

MULTI-PURPOSE

He uses them for everything
They often don't mean anything
He leaves them with nothing

Varying degrees of his
Needs or wants
Determine the depth
He is forced to
Or willing
To go

Gluttony being his
Favored sin
He feasts upon
Their emotional
Need

Savoring the flavor
Of collective fear
Seasoned lightly
With his own

Desire but a word
Ecstasy a button
Easily pushed
With a pressured curve

The same spot every time
No matter the shape
The age
The size

Something he mastered
Way back when
Delighting in the power
Necessary for his
Survival

Giving them everything
Filling them up
Leaving them empty
To drown in their
Sorrow

SHES GOT THE LOOK

She listened intently, as it was described to her; a single look packed with every emotion she refused to speak.

Offensive.
Threatening.
Intimidating.

Something until that moment, she was completely unaware of.

She heard herself apologizing; for something she had done unintentionally; a reaction she had unconsciously displayed; one that others had seen, did not like, and nonetheless commented on. She tried to reason, attempted to explain, but nothing appeased and so she apologized once more.

A defense mechanism.
A trigger response.
Raw, uninhibited, instinctual emotion.

Certainly not something she did on a whim, without reason or provocation; and certainly not intentional to cause such reaction; happening only when pushed; to the point where emotions automatic reaction is beyond conscious knowledge or control.

The only way she could define and describe it; falling on deaf ears that did not seek a reason, simply wanting to bring to light and condemn for.

A single look; nothing more. One that apparently, speaks louder than words.

She tried to reason this irrational response; what was expected in search of appeasement. Why such an issue was being made of nothing. But there was no rationale; only comparison came to mind, as she drove home that night...

Tell me; does a dog not bite when feeling threatened? Does a snake not strike when cornered? Does a child not wale in fury when feeling enraged, having no other way to express itself? Is she not a being of flesh, blood and feeling; not unlike that of yourselves? Or does her refusal to succumb to meaningless melodrama, remove her from your realm of the norm?

People fear, judge and ridicule that which they do not understand; yet none of whom she speaks, have ever taken the time to truly come to know her. Stop and consider what might have spurred her reaction; or consider for a second what might happen if her look were to be replaced with thoughts that spewed forth...

THE VISIT

He could see how tired she was, that day he happened upon her alone in the café; and though he purposely took his thoughts elsewhere, ignoring her completely, he knew from her body language that he'd once known so well, there was something amiss; and he couldn't help but wonder what was going on in her life that was causing such fatigue.

Years ago he'd gone away from her, removed her completely from the equation of his life; but that didn't stop him, from on occasion, seeing her shadow pass across his wall. Each time it happened, his perception shifting; re-instilling those truths and beliefs he'd discovered while in the presence of her; a presence he once believed was easy to shake, though part of him secretly yearned to hold onto.

While his real life was constantly in the forefront of his thinking, somewhere in the back of his mind lingered the life they had known; that driving light, filled with her laughter, dimmed by her cries, exploding with their passion; bringing something magical to his world of sameness.

His ability to sense her presence from miles away, clouding his memory on sun-dappled days; the one constant, through the years that had remained; though he still wasn't sure, if what he was feeling was real; or simply his imagination running wild, that caused him to linger, night after endless night. A vigil in the darkness, waiting for and willing her to come.

The rains came, followed by raging thunder and a fantastical lightening show, as he sat in the corner of the darkened room; waiting, watching, hoping; that she would not disappoint. He fell asleep in the chair somewhere around three, waking suddenly as a cool breeze, brushed gently across his flesh.

He opened his eyes and watched in silent fascination; as the misty shadow floated gracefully across the room; then as if willing it to happen, she slowly began to materialize.

She was wild-eyed in her misery, carrying the same tired and worn out expression he'd seen a few days before, etched across her beautiful face. He knew right then that he had called her to him; that she never would have come on her own. His heart overflowing, with the sudden feeling of guilt; for the pain he had caused, because of what together they had done.

He sat up a little straighter, unconsciously clinging to the arms of the chair; gathering courage, he spoke out to her. *"I don't blame you. I know you think I do; but I don't. I never did."*

She turned slowly, casting her gaze upon him; the veil of her so thin, that he could see right through it. In the blink of an eye, the span of a breath, she was upon him; face-to-face, as they once comfortably lay. She hovered in front of him, weightless; though he could feel her pressing down on him; searching his face, seeking truth in his eyes; as a single tear, sparkling like a jewel, dripped from hers; landing as a raindrop, upon his naked thigh.

He wanted to tell her that he missed her; that he worried and wondered of her constantly. That their time spent together had not been in vain; that a part of her, in his heart, would always remain. And while the words he still could not muster, the one thing she never ran dry of; the truth she saw clearly, in his green aging eyes.

THE FISH IS DEAD

It was one of those days; grueling, exhausting and quite frankly, unproductive. As if all I did the entire day, was shuffle stacks of papers from one end of the desk to the other and back. The end finally came, and with it the rains; nothing like rush hour traffic in a full blown storm to top off a perfectly miserable day!

My stomach reminded me about half way home that I hadn't taken a break for lunch and needed to eat. Too tired to even try to visualize the contents of my kitchen, I realized, as the line of cars in front of me suddenly came to a screeching halt, and I almost ate the ass end of a mini cooper, that I'd need to make an unwanted stop for food.

I knew I'd pay more, but didn't care, as I whipped into the parking lot of the Fresh Market. The thought of driving circles in Publix parking lot to try and find a place to park, then face the mass of shoppers, under row after endless row of glaring florescent lights, then argue with the check-out boy that I could manage just fine pushing my own cart to the car, made me want to gouge my eyes out.

So, into the Fresh Market I strolled; strolled in the pouring rain, with no umbrella and too tired to give a shit. The scent of the wicker baskets hanging from the ceiling, mingled with cinnamon and vanilla assaulted me the minute I crossed the threshold. The dim lights and soft music instantly calmed me, as I took my cart and began to stroll through fresh cut flowers and candle displays; choosing a lovely little hydrangea arrangement to adorn my kitchen table.

The gentleman at the meat counter waited patiently with a smile, as I tried to decide between chicken cordon bleu, or chicken ala Venezia. I turned to look; no one behind me, hmm…maybe I don't want chicken after all. He thanked me seven minutes later and told me to have a wonderful evening, then went back to whatever it was he was doing before I interrupted.

I wandered aimlessly, picking items that suited my fancy, sampling the pretty pink, perfectly chilled watermelon; my feet no longer hurting, the pounding in my head all but gone; enjoying the experience, wondering why I don't do all of my shopping here. Totally relaxed and nearly done; though I wasn't ready to leave the safe, comforting haven, to face the ugly rainy world that awaited me, just on the other side of those doors.

She made my decision for me, as I must have traveled too close to checkout territory, and she said with a bright and cheery smile, "I can help you over here Miss." MISS…how long has it been since anyone called me Miss!

Alrighty then; into her stall I turned.

She commented on my flowers, then proceeded to explain that even though I was purchasing reusable green bags that she was going to wrap my watermelon in plastic because she didn't want to get the rest of my things wet, just in case the container should leak. How very thoughtful, I mused to my self.

Then I don't know what happened; she started telling me about her last job at the pet store and how she got attached to one of the tropical fish, because every day when it saw her it swam to the side of the tank toward her and how one day she came in and it was dead. So upset she was over this dead fish that she was crying when her sister called her; but when her sister asked the cause of death, suggesting that perhaps it had drown, she reared her head back and released a raucous laugh that literally sent chills up my spine.

I suddenly noticed that during the story she was holding my snow peas hostage in her crazy clutches, and that most of my items still remained in the cart; only one green bag opened, and not even half full. Then I watched helplessly, as the other lone shopper turned and walked away; leaving me alone with the mad maven of blathering chatter.

Two items later she asks if I had a bad day, said I looked tired and worn out. Before I could respond with a righteous fuck you, she starts in about a new employee just recently transferred from another store; how mean he is; young guy that acts all fruity and that she's certain is gay. I took out my checkbook and asked her for a pen, prompting her to move her prejudice ass; as the ugly outside world didn't seem so ugly to me anymore.

On and on she went, until finally I looked at her and said, "did you ever think maybe that's why he's mean to you?" she looked at me and said, "Huh?" I repeated myself, more slowly than the first; "Did you ever think that maybe that's why he's mean to you?"

"Well, I don't know him or nothin', so he's got no reason to be treatin' me mean the way he does." She gave a slight jump when I exclaimed, "Exactly!" and pointed my finger at her.

"You don't know him, he doesn't know you, and yet because he doesn't act in a manner you've come to consider normal, acting instead in a way you consider 'fruity', you automatically make the assumption that he is gay?! What exactly about his behavior has led you to the position of assuming you know anything whatsoever about his sexual orientation?"

"His what?" I looked at her and shook my head in disgust. "His sexual preference; whether he prefers to have sexual relations with a person of the same or opposite gender." Just then a tidy little man with black rim glasses, who would have been perfectly fetching had his ensemble included a bowtie, came into view, making his way toward us and stopping to adjust some miscellaneous item at the end of the isle; obviously her manager.

He came into her line of vision, making his presence known and she immediately began scanning and bagging my remaining items. She gave me my total and I stroked a check. She thanked me by name as she handed me back my driver's license. "Well," I said, as I took it from her and put it back in my wallet; "are you some sort of psychic, or have you been called upon by a higher power to act as judge and jury?"

She leaned toward me and whispered, "We shouldn't talk about this anymore, ma'am." Oh, alright, suddenly I'm ma'am; no longer the friendly Miss! I leaned right back and said, "You're right, we shouldn't be, but I didn't ask for this conversation, and your coworker didn't ask to be judged and talked about behind his back; by a prejudice, no-count, blathering idiot. No wonder the fish is dead!"

I grabbed my bags and left her standing with her mouth agape, no doubt trying to decipher exactly what I had just said, then turned and nodded acknowledgment, when I heard clapping behind me and the pretty young cashier stood looking at me, with a grin that covered her whole face; obviously thankful that someone had put that old bag in her place.

THESE DAYS

Languid air
Laden with humidity
Wilting under the assault

Endless line
Twisting
Curving
All waiting to get inside

400 plus
Students alone
Not counting parents and sibs

Overzealous
Excited
Nervous
Shy

I stand in
Observance
With an unsuspecting eye

Listening to their
Exchanges
Hollow compliments throwing down

Cards
Trumping the
Jones'
Comparing exorbitant prices

Decked
To the nines
These women of leisure

In the same
Goddamn line

Ever the
Outcast
Seem to always have been

It bothered me
Once
Now I just shake my head

Observing their
Depth
Or rather lack thereof

Thinking to
My self

What
The
FUCK

MEANS TO AN END

With old patterns faltering in the wake of time, serving him less and less; desperation creeps, then slowly sets in.

Searching for something real to cling to; in a world of illusion and cheap parlor tricks; of which he created and has always dwelled.

Better to be an imaginary somebody, than a real no body; his platform, his soapbox, his mission, his salvation.

Spewing his gospel as weightless as smoke rings, growing bored with his half dozen converts; unable to stroke his monstrous ego; he sees only one place left to go.

One soul he touched. Upon a time was touched by. He refuses to release and let go. Disguised as forgiveness, he sets about his mission; back to the only arms left, that wait wide open.

Naïve and weak, yet privy to his ways; a masochist for certain, to take him back in. She is not the reason, but merely a convenience. Providing him shelter, buying him time; bringing him closer to where he believes salvation resides.

The beautiful butterfly, with delicate wings; once so fragile, easily ravaged; consumes his thoughts, still rules his darkness; and so true to predator form, of which he will always be, he sets about stalking, making connections; broadcasting his relation, as if guaranteeing him a position. Wasting time, sniffing and searching; for the butterfly has morphed, long ago taken flight.

And so time ticks on, for this wasted life; over educated and under achieved. When he could have soared to the greatest of heights; been a true inspiration, perhaps a revered master. But the only expertise, he can lay claim in the end; is leaving a trail of pain, in the wake of his disaster.

UNSETTLING REALIZATION

He'd reached a plateau; unable to put himself back out there; unwilling to be a participant in the games that most unconsciously played. He found it comforting that he was able to walk back in with no effort whatsoever. There was no uncomfortable adjustment period, no awkward beginning, no need to pretend he was someone he was not.

Days turned into weeks and then before he knew it, months had passed between them. What he'd first found endearing; the fact that she was the same as he had left her, so very long ago, suddenly began wearing on his nerves.

He sat across the table; watching, listening, unknowingly comparing; wondering how and why he'd ended up here again. So many years, so much life lived in between; and yet no growth or change, no matter how hard he tried, could he detect.

He noted their similarities; in physical appearance, as well as attitude. And as he looked at the elder, he could see exactly what she'd be in another twenty years; what she was turning into already.

The thought made him shudder; and he realized in that moment, that he wasn't willing to compromise the man he had become, for the girl she would always be.

FREEDOM

Today
I went walking
With the
Dead

That's
What I like
About the
South

A MOMENT IN TIME

It was a small southern town in the 1950's, just like every other, all across these "united" states. They were standing on the corner outside the drugstore; where the sign on the door read, "No Coloreds Allowed." Threes brothers in their late teens and early twenties, all of them the spitting image of their daddy; and the Tulle sisters, one of which had just agreed to marry the elder brother.

"What I wouldn't give, to walk in that store and order us up some celebratory soda's," Zachariah said with heartfelt enthusiasm; knowing full well that doing so would land him straight in the county jail, or worse. Miss May threw her arms around his neck and kissed him full on the lips. "There'll be plenty of time to celebrate once we tell our families the news."

With his heart overflowing with love and his mind in a heightened state of euphoria, Zachariah let out a walloping "WHOO-HOO," as he picked up his girl and swung her around in his arms. The crowd gathered in line outside the cinema, all turned to watch the spectacle; ever suspicious and wary of the ways of "the coloreds."

Zachariah set his bride-to-be gently on the ground, then proceeded to pick up his brothers in turn and do the same. Just then an elderly couple exited the drug store, and Zachariah ran up, grabbed the man's hand and shook it with enthusiasm, announcing that he was the happiest man in the world. The couple recoiled and the woman grabbed her husband by the arm. Zachariah paid no attention to the negative reaction, as there was nothing in the world could bring him down this day.

He leapt for joy, making his way toward the cinema, where he proceeded to shake the hands of everyone gathered in line. His brothers and the Tulle sisters, stood shaking their heads, laughing at his foolishness; delighting in their happiness. Then as if the world suddenly stopped spinning on its axes and began moving in slow motion, the shot rang out and Zachariah slowly fell backward to the ground. His body hit the pavement with a powerful thud, bounced a few inches back off the ground, then landed limp and lifeless.

The next morning the newspaper touted old man Henderson a hero; for single handedly stopping the colored boy, who as witness' claimed, had lost his mind, gone mad, and began attacking the crowd of innocent bystanders outside the Main Street Cinema.

MY SOUL SISTER

I see you suffering, and I wish there was something I could do for you.

I witness your pain, and my own heart aches.

I see you spiraling, faster each day; downward motion to nowhere land.

I wonder who'll be waiting when you reach the end.

Unsure what led you to this path; you no longer walk, but run these days.

The shift came sudden and without any warning.

Your sanity slipped and crazed madness set in.

You pushed aside all that was real; lost sight of your self completely.

Chasing that ever illusive sensation; known simply as euphoria.

You haven't a positive word to say; allowing negativity to swallow you whole.

I say these things, because I know this place; having visited a time or two.

Your beauty and intelligence still shines in your eyes; though clouded by your tears.

With love and understanding, I offer this prayer; that someday soon, you'll find your way home.

MAD WORLD

She made the mistake of reading the list of Top Ten News Headlines. Reminded, yet again, of the insanity that surrounds us; the human beasts we are forced to co-exist with. A truth that at times, is almost too much to bear.

Lab worker held in Yale student's slaying – Mom finds slain bodies of 2 kids, ex-husband – Case casts spotlight on sex offenders – Hofstra student recants rape story – Millionaire gets 8 years for sex with orphans – Teen could be charged in smaller L.A. fire – Bone found at Calif. kidnap suspects' home – Notre Dame sues ex-worker over $29,000 tip – Woman arrested for spanking stranger's child – Prison log: Execution trouble due to drug use

She finished the list, turned off the computer and gently shut the lid. Walked to her bedroom, closed the curtains, climbed into bed, pulled the covers over her head; and wept.

Some people laugh and call it cute.
Some people label her anti-social.
Some think she's naïve, lost in her own world.
Some call her a self-centered bitch.

Some say she's an overprotective mother.
Some advise she should cut the apron strings.
Some get it.
Some never will.

She didn't ask to be here. Wasn't an errant soul who mistakenly
happened into this world; sent here as punishment for behaving badly,
or waiting for that next big reincarnation, in search of a real adventure.
But she is.
Here.

That doesn't mean she has to like it. Doesn't mean that by being "one
with the universe," she must accept that being part of the "whole,"
means we are "all one." She's not certain if she will ever accept that as
truth. Perhaps that's why she's here now. Perhaps that's the one thing
that keeps bringing her back; over and over again.

She has a very clear vision of the duality of good and evil that lives
within each and every human being. Possesses an uncanny ability to
penetrate the façade, see behind the veil, and into the soul where good
and evil resides.
A gift?
 A curse?

Call it what you will, but its something she has lived with her entire
life. Defining and honing in her adulthood. Used as a tool to reason
and rationalize paths taken in her youth. Researching and recording
events predicted, premonitions seen, déjà vu witnessed.

Her path is a winding one. Her journey is of a spiritual nature. Not in
search of God, for she knows where He dwells, but rather to obtain a

better understanding of the why's and how's of this material world, as well as the afterworld and those who dwell in between the two. Knowing for certain that when we reach the highest realm of being, we will be shown the ultimate reality; when everything else leading to it, is nothing but illusion; an illusion that all too often is filled with real life monsters, who take lives and destroy souls.

There is a very real battle of good and evil, existing in all corners of the world, every single minute of every single day. Well aware of the ever-present threat, she does not wear blinders because she's too weak or uncaring to handle the truth of the world. She does it out of necessity; for her own personal survival.

She is unable to return the gift she was given; to lift the curse and see only what she chooses; incapable of numbing herself to the truth within the illusion, by allowing herself to be spoon fed images that television executives and the media think we need to see and hear, by simply tuning in and zoning out. It doesn't work that way for her. But, oh, how she sometimes wishes it did…

EMPTY

Just not feeling it today.

Didn't feel it yesterday.

Tomorrow's not lookin' too good either.

LOCKDOWN

Echoes swirl
Through hallowed
Halls

Bouncing off doors
Inside my
soul

Meaningless words
Wrapped in
Illusion

A singular voice
Bent on spiritual
Intrusion

Bolt the door
Against his
Dark

Shut my eyes
Seek thy
Light

FORTUNE COOKIE

"Your life is like a Kaleidoscope."

I'll take that!

DEPICTION

There comes a certain "feel," no matter where you happen to be, whenever his thoughts turn in your direction.

It starts at the basic level of the flesh; like the cool breeze on a crisp autumn night; tantalizing and chilling all at once.

Your blood pressure rises, heart rate increases, as he sends invisible waves of desire, cascading in your direction.

At the sound of his voice, a chemical reaction triggers, and suddenly you are seized; with a mix of exhilaration and excitement like none other you have ever known.

A connection is what he seeks; the ability to reach out and snatch you from reality; pulling you into his realm of illusion; with nothing more than his thoughts and voice.

Once he connects, the feeding begins; everything you want to hear, anyone you want him to be; larger than life, too good to be true; having searched for eternity and now loving only you.

Before you can blink, you are on a downward spiral; surrendered completely while careening out of control.

He drains you empty, while filling you up; taking every scrap offered, pillaging the rest while you dream.

Making his exit as quickly as he comes; a puddle of nothing, you remain on the floor. Left alone, to sift through the pain; cloaked in his filthy blanket of noir.

SIGNS

The first letter
Of the first
Word

Put down and
Purged

The stroke of
Midnight

All Hallows Eve

He always
Believed
Her to be a
Witch

Leaving him damned
And cursed

One thousand and one
Her number on
The list

Nameless
Faceless
Meaningless
Conquests

The exact number
Final word count
At the end of first
Go-round

Everything flowing
Coming with ease
Alignments just right
For slaying the
Dead

BABY DID A BAD, BAD THING

She stood at the sink with a handful of paper towels and a bottle of liquid soap, scrubbing herself until she bled; desperately trying to remove his scent; but no matter how hard she tried, she could still smell him on her. She looked in the mirror; her face a complete blur; her smeared mascara giving her eyes the illusion of black hollow demon sockets; seen through tears of self-loathing. She dug in her bag looking for a barrette; her hair a wild jumbled mass of curls, from his grubby fingers running through it. She stopped short when she saw the envelope; opened it slowly and stared at the three thousand dollar bills.

Mother fuck; what had she done...

MUTUAL ADMIRATION SOCIETY

Of mutual admiration
I never truly was
A member of his
Society

I wonder
If anyone but him
Ever really is

ONE STEP BEYOND

Finding the capacity
To bend without
Breaking

A willingness to
Change
Or be changed

Some times
Often times
Easier said than
Done

About the Author

Jill describes herself as a word-weaver, story teller, truth-seeker; who finds solace in putting her thoughts to words and sharing with all those who would listen. An accomplished award winning author, whose talents span several genres; Jill is one of those people who have found what she loves to do and keeps plugging away, despite the odds.

A genuine love of the craft and a satisfying creative outlet is what keeps her turning out one book after another. Her natural ability to light a fire of compassion as well as heart-pounding excitement has been extolled time and again by reviewers and readers alike.

All books are written under pen name J.A. Terry and are available wherever books are sold. For more information, visit her website at jillterry.com. For a list of upcoming releases, visit www.pandorasboox.org.

Other titles by Jill Terry

Fragments from Being
Exposed
Full Circle
MACUMBA
Shadows of my Soul
Premonition
Destination Unknown

Anthologies:

Coffee Break Poetry
Unrestrained

Pandora's Boox

Filling the Box - One Story at a Time...

www.pandorasboox.org

www.ingramcontent.com/pod-product-compliance
Lightning Source LLC
Chambersburg PA
CBHW020640030726
47498CB00002B/292